RAIN OF FIRE

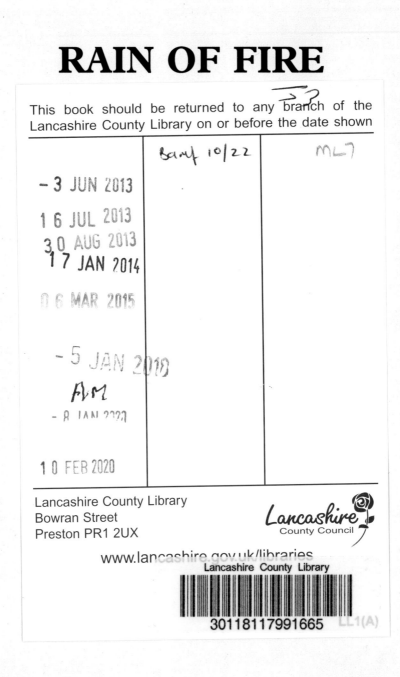

This book should be returned to any branch of the
Lancashire County Library on or before the date shown

Banf 10/22	ML7

- 3 JUN 2013

1 6 JUL 2013

3 0 AUG 2013

1 7 JAN 2014

0 6 MAR 2015

- 5 JAN 2019

AM

- 8 JAN 2020

1 0 FEB 2020

RAIN OF FIRE

MERLE CONSTINER

SAGEBRUSH
Large Print Westerns

First published in Great Britain by ISIS Publishing Ltd.
First published in the United States by Ace Books

Published in Large Print 2012 by ISIS Publishing Ltd.,
7 Centremead, Osney Mead, Oxford OX2 0ES
by arrangement with
Golden West Literary Agency

British Library Cataloguing in Publication Data
Constiner, Merle.
Rain of fire.
1. Western stories.
6. Large type books.
I. Title
813.5'4–dc23

ISBN 978–0–7531–8996–2 (pb)

Printed and bound in Great Britain by
T. J. International Ltd., Padstow, Cornwall

11799166

CHAPTER
ONE

The transient was an enigma, and vaguely alarming, even to this village of Iraville which had seen more than its quota of disturbing visitors. For one thing, he gave his name with a dry grin as the whim prompted him: Pickett, Sackett, Volmer, and even Ferguson.

For another, he said he was headed north, north of Blue Gravel Crossing, bent on buying horses. For three days he had been loafing about the place, sitting on his heels wherever there was a patch of thin shade, doing nothing, staring, dreadfully alone. Sulphur-yellow travel dust powdered his thong hatband, his rundown boots, his gaping empty holster.

And that was the strangest thing of all about him, perhaps. He wore a holster, low-tied, but empty.

He was thirty, maybe, of middle height, gaunt and sinewy. His eyes were an unfriendly purple, almost dreamy, and he was so scornful of his personal appearance that his uncut hair grew in a ringleted beaver tail down the back of his neck, about a half inch over the rim of his frayed porcupine-quilled vest.

Respectable ranchers and townsmen, listening to his story about buying those horses up north, didn't look too happy at its sound. Up north you could buy wonderful horses all right, and dirt cheap, if you were patient and put out the proper feelers. Stolen horses.

Iraville, in the west central part of Montana, was a real border town, though the border was wide, flexible and hard to put your finger on. Some distance north was the Musselshell River and north of the Musselshell was the Milk River. The terrain between these two rivers, and the belt approaching them north and south, for that matter, was hard-case country and worse. The patches of wilderness which clotted it were black with the phantoms of vanished men, and even its bleak tense towns were areas of *no-strangers-wanted*.

There was no badge nearer to Iraville than at Stapleton, the county seat, twenty-odd miles to the south. Just over a swelling north of Iraville was the loop of a wet-weather stream. Horse tracks and a few wagon tracks led down to it between a couple of hard earth hogbacks. This was Blue Gravel Crossing. If you were foolish enough to make that crossing, you were on your own.

Iraville was on the plain, and any way you looked out from it was grass, red-brown like tundra in winter, greasy green in rippling crest waves in summer. Roundabout, the circling horizon appeared always thread-thin and very close. The wind-pounded, sun-seared village itself was a scattering of a few hovels and huts only. There were two one-room saloons and a store.

The store was owned and run by Joe Fane and his wife Betty. Fane had spent his boyhood here, when there was nothing to talk to but family, and nothing to play, unless you wanted to play war party, or renegade

2

— alone. It was when Fane was about fourteen, on a solitary walk with his father's spare six-gun and a box of St. Louis cartridges, that a bolt of lightning hit him, a sort of seizure, and he fell in love with weapons. From then on he was really gun-gone.

Both Fane and Betty were devoted to the country. They saw the population thickening with, when you came right down to it, a pretty good class of citizens, some with plow-handle callouses or lariat burns on their palms.

The country was growing and prospering. The store was on the verge, on the very edge, of growing and prospering too. The store was an obsession. Childless, it was almost like a child to them.

Tuesday morning, just after breakfast, Joe Fane had left for Bent Skillet hills, a circle of wooded knobs about ten miles out of Iraville. He had gone into the Bent Skillet country to deliver a chicken-dog. This particular chicken-dog was part hound and part terrier, and very lovable. He had taken it in part trade from a farmer south of town on a brace of ax heads. It was a funny kind of deal but you had to relax rules sometimes, and the farmer now was a loyal and solid customer. Few people that lived in the open spaces had hencoops. Most just let their chickens run loose and forage for themselves. This made a slight problem, of course, when a fowl was wanted for a meal, or a church affair. Running the fowl down and catching it was hard, so many a home kept a dog trained for this purpose. A good chicken-dog would run down a fowl and bring it in gently, in a careful mouth, unharmed.

Because this one was lovable, and Betty and Fane wanted it to have a good master, and because they knew of just such a man in the Bent Skillet country, and because they thought, too, that it might be a good idea to socialize a little and cultivate a few new customers in that area, Joe had set off. He had run into a chain of parties being given for a bride, had found himself unable to break away.

The stranger came to town on Tuesday, while Joe Fane was away. That Thursday night, Fane returned and walked his team of little mares down Iraville's rutted Main Street, down the alley, and unhitched his buckboard in the lean-to behind the store. This done, the mares groomed and fed, he passed through the heavy slab door into the room behind the store.

This was their bedroom and kitchen. It was bad judgement, they decided, to spend money on a cabin. Every penny they could lay their hands on was doubled back into stock for the store. Through a doorway which had no door on its jambs, Fane could see the store out front: pig lead, harness, ready-made candy, muslin, the store which was just beginning to mushroom, the store they both felt in their hearts would one day become the biggest mercantile emporium north of the county seat.

Betty Fane sat in a big green easy chair looking over a fine print catalog on variety hardware. She was a small girl, scarcely out of her teens, with coffee-colored hair and lustrous clear blue eyes; she seemed from an entirely different race of humans than her rolling, muscular, red-haired husband. As soon as he entered, even before he could get words out of his mouth to

4

greet her, even before he kissed her, she had arisen and put two pork chops in a pan. He wiped grime and sweat from his mouth, splay handed, and kissed her. She brought the coals in the stove, magically, to the proper heat, went out front to the store and returned with a scoop of hominy from the hominy keg, a can of tomatoes, a few cloves and an aromatic pinch of freshly ground pepper. While she mixed and layered these over the pork chops, and put the pan over the fire, she asked, "Anything happen?"

"I almost got married again at a wedding by a drunken preacher who mistook me for the bridegroom."

"My," she said. "How did the bridegroom take it?"

"Hard to really tell," said Fane, sinking into a chair. "But there was a minute there — before they got it straightened out — when I suspected, just suspected, you understand, that he was wildly hopeful."

She looked at him to see if he was serious. He wasn't. "You men!" she said.

"Anything happen here?" he asked.

"Yes," she said. "There was a stranger around a couple of days ago. Didn't seem inclined to give his name. Said it wasn't important. He wanted to see the Old Man Mattock gun."

Fane perked up. Another sideline of his business, other than general trading and bartering, was gun collecting — swapping, selling, buying. He had gravitated into this because he couldn't seem to help himself. It was more than a hobby with him, it was sort of a strange compulsion.

His collection of these secondhand guns was here in their living quarters, in a pine cabinet in a corner of the room. He sat silently a moment, thinking about the Old Man Mattock gun. It was his most recent acquisition.

Old Man Mattock, a rawhide and bear-claw desperado of a generation ago, had come out of retirement last month to rob a bank — single-handed!

But a farm boy in town to get a tooth pulled, shot him out of his saddle as the old man, trying to escape, tried to ride the boy down at a hitching rack.

They flattered the boy, and gave him the old man's gun, and kept the bank reward. Fane, sensing the desperado would certainly have a fine weapon, looked the boy up at his father's homestead, and bought it.

It was a new gun, of the latest model, and this surprised Fane. It no longer had factory butt plates, but home-made butt plates of some milky-golden colored wood, like birch, crosshatched with a file edge in a pattern of diamonds.

As soon as Fane got out of sight of the farmhouse, and the smoke from the farmhouse chimney, he tried the gun out against an improvised target set up by a clay bank.

His nerve ends couldn't seem to adjust themselves to the new butt, and every time he tried a rapid draw he fumbled it a little — just a little, but that was enough. He came to the conclusion that the gun was a death trap, and that Old Man Mattock had followed someone's ignorant advice, and that the weapon was actually an eccentric.

"Did he ask for the Old Man Mattock gun by name?" said Fane.

"Yes," said Betty.

"Did you show it to him?"

"Yes."

"What then? Did he look excited?"

"Look excited? That man? Hah."

"Well, what?" asked Fane, feeling excited himself.

"He wanted to buy it," she said. "Offered me twice its value."

"Did you sell it?"

"No," she said putting the savory plate of hominy and pork on the table.

"Why not?" said Fane.

"I've just told you," she said. "He offered me twice its value, and he didn't look to me like a man that would make a mistake like that."

"So he walked away," said Fane quietly.

"Not exactly," she said. "I explained to him that bread and cookies were my sideline, that the guns were yours, and that you were out of town."

"And that satisfied him?"

"Seemed to. He said to tell you he was rooming at the hotel."

"Hotel?" said Fane, surprised. "When did that happen? When did we get a hotel?"

"That seems to be what he calls the old Fort Smith and Fort Benton stables." She grinned.

"Why that's four miles out of town," said Fane. "And nothing lives under that rotted roof anymore but rats and mice and Yellowstone Johnson with his one-man-consumption whiskey still."

Fane went to the cabinet, unlocked it, and took out the gun they had been discussing. "I'll finish my supper when I get back. This has got me nervous. I've got to get it settled."

She nodded and watched him go. She understood him by now.

At first, because the distance was so short, he thought he'd walk and loosen his legs and enjoy the blue summer night and the white moon, but then, because he wanted to get to bed, he changed his mind at the last minute and saddled Blue, his rangy saddle mount.

The moon was hanging high over the plain behind scudding clouds when Blue walked through the buffalo grass up to the structure which had once been the F.S.&F.B. office, quarters, with stables attached. The buildings were ramshackle, low, squalid in the gray-silver light and streaked with musty black shadow. A single window showed light, red-gold through glass.

Fane dismounted and tied his gelding to the root of a sawed-off stump; the company public hitching rack had gone long ago to fire Yellowstone's hidden still. A little dog, about the size of a sick squirrel, came flying out of nowhere, barking and yelping his ill-tempered head off. Fane strode past the dog opened a sagging door, and entered the building. Out of a battery of sagging doors, he chose the one a hands-breadth from the golden window. He found himself in a small room.

There were two men in the room, seated at a table — an oldster in rags and tatters, and a younger man, hard-faced, sardonic-faced, in a frayed quilled vest and an empty holster. The old man was Yellowstone; the other was a stranger. There was a rumpled gunny sack on the floor in a corner — a pallet, Fane guessed.

This was the hotel and this was the man's room. At the moment, Yellowstone was showing his guest a rather biggish snake skull, dull white, which seemed to be all eye sockets and curved fangs in the lamplight.

The old man was talking: "I got it from a litty-bitty lost tribe of Indians tucked away in the heart of the Wind River Mountains. None of the braves of this tribe would be without one. They ain't nothing to equal one as a pocket-piece charm. It'll ease you into a world o' romance, if your taste turns that way, turn aside arrows and bullets, and will keep you soberer at a drinkin' bout better'n a bellyful of lard. I had to go through three days ceremonial torture and battle the chief with a bowie knife in each hand before they awarded me one. As much as it tears my heartstrings to part with it, I'll leave you have it for eighty-five cents."

They paid no attention to Fane, either of them.

The man in the quilled vest said gravely, "Being a mortal man, the advantages you enumerate sound mighty attractive. But I'm afraid, much as it tears at my heartstrings, that I'm going to have to turn down yore nacherally reasonable proposition. Besides, look at those fangs! I'd be afraid to tote it around on me. It might bite me through my pocket!"

"It's dead," said Yellowstone.

9

"That's what you say," said the other man skeptically. "Maybe yes, maybe no. Snakes can be mighty sneaky."

Exasperated, Yellowstone said, "But this is jest a skull!"

"I'll grant that," said the other. "But a mean snake with a grudge against mankind might go to a lot of trouble to trick you."

Turning to Fane, he said, "I don't believe I caught yore name?"

"Joe Fane," said Fane. "I run the store in Iraville. My wife directed me here. I've got an item to sell."

"Seems like tonight just about everyone has an item to sell," said the man, his eyes twinkling.

But Fane, dog-tired and hungry, was in an ugly mood and went up in flame. He said, "An hour before dawn I climbed into a buckboard. All forenoon, I rode over rocks. All afternoon, I cooked in an oven of prairie sun. Just now, as soon as I got your message, I came here. I left my supper half eaten." He spoke as offensively as he could.

The muscles of the man's cheeks remained relaxed and expressionless, but his purple eyes hardened and for a split second seemed to cloud, as his mind balanced and counterbalanced the judgement, as he decided whether or not to accept Fane's belligerent tone.

He spoke to the old man. "I don't want the snake skull, but you can add eighty-five cents to my room bill, just for the hell of it. Okay? Now would you leave us alone? Mr. Fane and I have a little business to transact."

Good-humoredly, Yellowstone left the room.

10

The stranger said, "Mr. Fane, it's a pleasure and honor to meet you. I never heard anyone say you were the world's quickest shot, but they all agree the way you find your target within any reasonable range dries a man's gullet just to behold."

"*They* all agree?" said Fane. "Who and where?"

"Gentlemen you never heard of, in places you never heard of."

"I don't believe it," said Fane, paralyzed at the enormity of the idea.

"Did you bring it?" asked the man.

"Bring what?" asked Fane, suddenly very cautious indeed.

"My gun," said the man simply.

"No," said Fane. "I brought Old Man Mattock's gun."

"That's my gun," said the man. "He stole it from me the night before that kite-flying, rabbit-trapping, jackknife-trading homestead kid blew him into a better world. I've just run it down to you. I've got to have it. You know what I'm talking about if you're a marksman yourself. It's got my balance like I was poured into it."

"I know," said Fane. "Like father and son."

"Now I've told you that," the man said, "you've got me in a forked stick. How much?"

"If you say it's yours," said Fane, "and I believe you, there's no cost whatever. A man has to have his own gun. And besides, I don't deal in stolen goods."

The stranger smiled, and it was a warm thrilling thing to observe. He said, "I know more about you right now than any other mortal on the face of this globe."

"That I'm honest?"

"That you're honest is a certainty. That you can be trusted is a conviction. And men like me live or die by these convictions. Would you like to know my name?"

"No."

"I was baptized Alexander John Martin, but that got mislaid somewhere. I'm more generally known as Arapaho. I'm a sort of drifter, you might say."

"There are dozens of drifters known as Arapaho," said Fane. "And Kiowa, and Apache, and Comanche, and just about everything Indian."

"Now, is that so?" said Arapaho, looking amused.

Fane laid the gun on the table. "Now we're finished," he said, "I've got to go."

"You think I'm a robber, like Old Man Mattock."

"I don't think anything. One way or the other. I've got two pork chops and some cold hominy to finish."

"I'm on the gun, all right," said Arapaho. "And have been since my old man dusted me off the place. But I'm not a thief."

"You're still alive. That means you must be good."

"If I said I was good today. I'd be dead tomorrow," said Arapaho. "Get a big head in my business and you'd better start pricing your own coffin. And I've got to stay alive, at least until I get up to Bruce Galdecker's *B-reversed B*." He smiled. "That's in the contract."

When he could speak, Fane said. "Are you talking about Bruce Baldecker and *B-reversed B* up at Split Butte?"

"Yes."

"Are you one of these 'for hire' gunthrowers?" said Fane. "Is that what you are?"

"Well, I don't work free."

As though trying to convince himself, Fane said, "The Bruce Baldecker I've got in mind would never hire a professional to salt somebody's pelt. He'd do it himself."

"Well, this time he did."

Aghast, Fane stood mute. The dry old building seemed to creak. Night noises came to him from the prairie — "But why?" he said.

"He's got trouble."

"What trouble?"

"For one thing," answered Arapaho, "his neighbor is bringing in men, professionals like me, against him."

After a long pause, Fane said, "These are touchy days back in the hinterlands, back in the new country. A lot of swaggering goes on. Many a man makes a show of force, then does nothing about it. Maybe it will all blow over, whatever it is."

"Sure," said Arapaho, absently, agreeably.

"Can I sit down a minute?" asked Fane, "and hear a little more about this?"

"I owe you that much and a heap more," said Arapaho.

CHAPTER
TWO

Scarcely an hour elapsed before Fane was back at his store, his return slow and preoccupied. The story Arapaho had told him was a short one, short and worrying.

Baldecker's neighbor, a man from the east coast, young, unscrupulous, ambitious, was hell-bent on making a spectacular success of himself for his friends back home, and, over a period of time, working carefully in a pattern, had laid out a doctored sequence of incidents for the Split Butte community making it appear that Baldecker was constantly imposing upon him. This done, he was moving into the final phase of his plan and had brought in a crew of killers from Colorado. His ultimate goal was simply a *B-reversed B* land grab, and Baldecker, feeling the avalanche about to break over him, was trying wildly — and not too sanely, thought Fane — to save himself. An old-timer, trusting humanity, he had been outmaneuvered, outwitted, and was on the verge of being outfought.

Fane told Betty all about it as he cleaned up the cold hominy on the chipped blue enamel plate.

She saw that he was terribly upset, sensed that he was scarcely within the realm of reason himself as he rambled on, and was careful not to distress him further by word or gesture.

Bruce Baldecker, in Fane's boyhood, had been a close friend of Fane's father, until a dispute had smacked up between them. One thing though, maybe because of old ties, maybe because of the sanity of their wives, they had the common sense to separate. Fane's father stayed in his sod cabin. Baldecker moved up to Split Butte. Later they heard word of him and how he had prospered.

And now a strange thing happened in the Fane cabin. As time passed, memories surged into their minds — Mr. Fane's, Joe's, his mother's — and their eyes softened when word was heard of him, and the hate softened to love once more.

It was an absurd sense of guilt, a vague feeling of remorse, with nobody actually to blame, that fogged up Fane's thinking now.

"He's in trouble, all right," said Betty, trying to be sympathetic, but careful not to rip the tranquil film of control through which Fane spoke. "Times have changed, haven't they?"

"Times have changed, and gunmen have changed," said Fane. "When Bruce was young, these mercenaries were mainly wild kids. Now they are the butchers that stand behind their block and pass out whatever stew meat and soup bones you've enough money to pay for. Arapaho says that Bruce, through an old friend, a saloonkeeper, has hired a mad-dog killer name Crezavent and himself to stand up against these four Colorado experts."

Betty said, "Two heavy men on one side, Arapaho and Crezavent, against these four Colorado killers. It seems like uncomfortable odds. I'd say your friend Arapaho just doesn't care."

"Sure he cares," said Fane. "But it's my guess he's all man."

They sat there and stared at each other, reading each other's thoughts.

"Don't, Joe," she said. "Please."

"Betty," he said, "I know you're tired. Working behind the counter all day is no joke. But will you do me a favor?"

"Why, certainly."

"Get a feed sack. Go out front and collect a few things for it. Say four or five onions, a couple of cans of salmon, a hunk of dried beef about twice as large as your fist, some cornmeal, about a pound of those wild cherry candy lozenges we just got in, a little bacon . . ."

"You're going with him."

"I have to," he said unhappily.

"Well, I'd rather have you dead than tormented," she said, and got to her feet.

He sat moodily, slouched, his blunt strong fingers locked over his lean iron-hard stomach.

Out front, from the store, came little sounds made by her hands as she got together the provisions.

Candy, he thought, *salmon*. If it's going to be a one-way trip we might as well do it in sinful luxury.

Within twenty minutes, Fane arrived on his gelding and feed sack at the old F.S.&F.B. buildings, still showing lamplight, to find Arapaho already gone. Yellowstone was wordy, but when you came right down to it, he had nothing to tell but this: The nice stranger had payed his bill and moved on.

Fane got this information at the doorstep without leaving his saddle. He thanked the old man, turned his gelding, and headed north.

He overtook Arapaho on the moon-frosted prairie, about a quarter of a mile south of Blue Gravel Crossing.

Arapaho, with the ears and night eyes of a hunter, had heard him coming, and had even identified him, for he was sitting his saddle, statue-still, relaxed, waiting. He said in a voice deep with friendship and satisfaction, "Don't tell me you came along to take care of me?"

"I came along to take care of Bruce Baldecker," said Fane. "He was once my father's closest friend."

"That doesn't surprise me too much," said Arapaho. "In the old days, in Baldecker's day, just about every man belonged to some network or other of friendship-loyalty. If you ride with me, though, you've got to understand one thing to start with: There's one head man here, it's me. It has to be that way. I won't have you fetch and carry like an Apache and his slave boy, but I'm the one that says *yes* when the yes time comes, and *no* when the no time comes. And that's what you do."

Fane moved his gelding up, so that they were sitting girth crowded to girth. In a soft but friendly voice, he said, "The only one that says yes and no to me is my wife, back at Iraville. And even then, sometimes, we spend a good many night hours talking it over, coming to that conclusion."

After the briefest of hesitations, Arapaho said, "Well, I've trusted you this far, I think I'll take a chance and trust you all the way. Are you going to want any pay for this?"

Fane scorned to answer.

"I had to ask you," said Arapaho. "With me it's a business. We had to get that straight. I had to know whether to expect you to pop up and lay it into me for half of my own personal fees later. I ain't the only lunatic that's chose this as a trade. How did I know you didn't have secret aspirations along that line yourself?"

"Well, I don't," said Fane curtly.

"Let's move on," said Arapaho.

It was there, all right, the Old Man Mattock's gun in his holster. Fane could recognize it even in the moon glow, with its wooden crosshatched butt.

Blue Gravel Crossing, when they crossed it shortly after, seemed merely like a boggy mud hole between two dirt hogbacks in the moon shadows, and the strip of arid earth on its yonder side seemed like any other Montana soil, but both of them, Fane and his companion, knew that they had left one thing behind them and were now a part of something quite different.

Gray dawn light, silver first then flowing into red and bronze, guided them through a seemingly endless wave of aspens and unexpected reaches of sage. By noon the aspens had gone into arid chokeberry and dry hawthorn, but the sage began to predominate.

They had their midday meal by a little stream of sweetwater hardly the size of a strand of yarn at the base of a small rolling rise, with ridges of pie-crust-looking gulch clay on either side of them. It was here, as he was finishing his coffee, that Arapaho spoke to Fane for the first time of their mutual project at any length, in any detail.

He said they were riding two days north, to a town named Polton which they would circle — for this Polton was a terror — and end up eventually at the shack of a man named Grissle. Then they would be in the Split Butte country, not too far from the *B-reversed B* place.

"Is this Grissle a friend of yours?" asked Fane.

"He's a friend of the dollar," replied Arapaho. "His shack will be our rendezvous with Crezavent."

"I've been wondering a little about this Crezavent, to tell the truth," said Fane. "You gave me a kind of terrible picture of him. Is he like you?"

"He follows the same trade, but otherwise no, I hope. Wait until you meet him."

"What's his main fault?" asked Fane curiously.

"He kills men."

This seemed like a strange comment under the circumstances, so Fane remained silent.

Arapaho said indifferently, "He'll no doubt kill me sometime, and maybe even you. Who knows?"

"Me?" said Fane, not particularly alarmed, but startled. "Why?"

"Maybe you'll remind him of some railroad man he met eight years ago that he didn't like. Or maybe he'll mumble something to you you didn't quite catch and ask him to repeat it, and smile when you ask him, or maybe just because you're extra nice to him. He'll get the idea you're laying it on because really you hate him and are plotting his downfall in secret."

"You mean he's crazy as a bedbug?"

"You said it, I didn't."

The moon was in the dark when they passed the town of Polton, off to their left. It lay in a shallow basin, surrounded by low, linked, wooded hills. "Stay away from it," warned Arapaho.

They reached Grissle's shack in the scorching yellow dust of a hot day's afterglow. It was a funny kind of a shack, more cave to Fane's eye. Vines and grass roots drooped down from the overhang above it, nearly fringing the little rabbit-hole doorway. On either side of the door-hole were a few derelict looking objects, a limping legged grindstone, a bench, a clutter of steel traps, rusting from slovenly neglect. There was no sign of any human.

Arapaho, his lean hand on his pommel, called: "It's me, Arapaho!"

Faintly, from a short distance, a voice called back: "Here, over here, son!"

They rode up the slope of a hill to their left, through its nestlike crown of cedars, wind pounded to eerie shapes by the endless brutality of the prairie air drafts, and down its hither side into a clump of surprisingly lush cottonwoods.

A creek flowed into the grove. On the near bank of the water's edge was dirty old man with silver unshaven stubble like lint in blotches on his cheeks. He was bending over a fish trap which he had just hoisted from the pool, a home-made contrivance of saplings, shaped in a long roomy tube, an open cone inward at either end, weighted within by rocks. Along with the rocks was a rotting elk haunch, the bait. He was extracting the day's catch, a turtle, a writhing mass of crayfish, and an assortment of flopping fish of varying sizes. Each small fish he threw back into the pool, saying, "Grow up. And don't pilfer no more o' my bait until you'll fit in a man's mouth."

Arapaho said, "Grissle, howdy. It appears I beat Crezavent."

"He beat you," said the oldster. "Got here two days before yestiddy, and went on."

"Went on?" said Arapaho.

"He's a man that can't bear to wait," said Grissle.

"Alone?" said Arapaho.

"He's a feller that ain't never alone," said Grissle. "And you should know it as well as anybody."

When Arapaho said nothing, but simply looked chill and blank, the old man said, "I suppose you'll want proof?"

"From an ordinary man, no," said Arapaho, thinly, "but from you, yes."

And he'd better get it, too, thought Fane, for this was an ominous situation.

The old man dug into the pocket of his bib overalls and came out with a scrap of brown wrapping paper. Arapaho read it and passed it on to Fane. Script in heavy pencil, so illiterate it was barely readable, said: *Arapaho — am moving on. Join me up there.*

"What are you having for supper?" Arapaho asked the oldster.

"Skillet sizzled crawfish tails, if you so desire them."

"I don't desire them," said Arapaho.

"Then you don't know good eatin'," said the old man.

"How about some of that cat?" suggested Arapaho.

"Then cat it is," said the old man promptly. "You're the buyer, I'm just the seller. Catfish supper. At ten dollars per serving."

"Ten dollars!" said Fane, outraged.

"Mighty big servings," said Grissle. "I guarantee one will hold you."

"But ten dollars!" repeated Fane.

"You're buyin' lots more than catfish for that ten dollars," reminded the old man grimly. "You're buying my loss of memory."

"And that comes high," said Arapaho. "Let's go back to the shack and wash up."

They left the old man in the grove and rode up the hillside. At the top, in the cedars, Fane said, "Did Crezavent write that?"

"Yes," said Arapaho with finality. "No argument there."

"Then why do you look so troubled?"

"I always look troubled when something happens I can't get through my thick meathead."

22

"You mean because he left?"

"I mean because he come back."

He pointed down the hillside.

Now, before Grissle's shack was a tough looking piebald pony and on the bench by the shack's door sat a man, smoking a cigarette, his boots off, his feet frog-flat in the dust. "Crezavent," said Arapaho.

As he rode up, Fane added him up as well as he could, like he would a complicated six months' rancher's bill. At first glance, he looked like just about any man you might try to remember, but couldn't quite: middle height, average weight, stiff tea-colored duck pants, one gun, one gun only, and a stomach as flat as a board. Then, as you came closer, you saw that dreadful laxness, that unnatural serenity in such a queer frozen degree that, to Fane's mind, could scarcely indicate anything but madness.

He got up as they joined him. To Arapaho, he said, "Who's this?"

Arapaho introduced Fane briefly indeed. "I've taken him in with us," he said. "He's not a lightning draw, but he's a dead shot."

"There's no law that says he can't be both at the same time," said Crezavent. "You say you hired him?"

"Yes, in a manner of speaking," said Arapaho.

"Then fire him in the same manner of speaking," said Crezavent.

"You'll have to come out with something better than that," said Arapaho, tightening. "Why?"

"For one thing, Bruce Baldecker has eat dirt and sold out and merged with the other feller. It's all over."

Fane felt befuddled.

Arapaho said gently to him, "If Crezavent says it's all over, it's all over." To Crezavent, he said, "They were old friends."

Crezavent said, "Whoppin' big sums of money changed hands. Cigars as long as ox tails was lit and puffed and toasts was drunk to let bygones be bygones. Gunslingers, such as certain gentlemen from Colorado and yours truly, were called troublemakers and give their walking papers with ever' hand agin 'em and the law called in to chase 'em out."

"Then we'd better pass up that catfish supper," said Arapaho thoughtfully. "And burn us some horseshoes heading south."

Crezavent nodded. "No doubt about it," he said. "What you got in that sack tied to your cantle, Mr. Fane?"

"A little food," said Fane. "Just a few traveling provisions."

"Then we'll all go together," said Crezavent. "The last time I seen victuals of any kind was sundown yesterday when I caught and ett six grasshoppers."

"Together?" said Fane with a frown. "Well, I don't know."

The air became suddenly charged with tension.

"He always says well-I-don't-know when he means yes," explained Arapaho.

"Let's hear it from him," said Crezavent.

"Yes," said Fane though the words were like gall, trusting Arapaho's guidance, knowing this was no time to start a fracas.

24

CHAPTER
THREE

They burned those horseshoes, all right, heading south and it was just after daybreak on the second day following that the skinny sheriff, a stranger, stopped them at gunpoint and arrested Crezavent. Just Crezavent, neither Fane nor Arapaho.

They were riding along at that professional distance-eating pace set by Arapaho.

They had just crossed an area of old burn-over, now sprouting rank dusty weeds, and were passing through sandstone rubble when a trio of men rose up in front and on either side of them. It had been planned and executed so expertly that there was no defense.

Their leader, a tall skinny man with a sheriff's badge, with a harsh flinty face and bright little beady eyes, said, "Build like a bobcat. Sleepy looking. Stiff pale yellow pants, middle height. You're him, all right. Charles Fentress Crezavent. Correct?"

Insultingly, Crezavent didn't bother even to answer.

The sheriff snapped on handcuffs. And Fane had to admit this man was a real professional himself. Those handcuffs appeared and went on Crezavent's wrists with the speed and complete lack of show — like a man reaching for a table fork.

"Well, goodbye, boys," said Crezavent. "You won't see me again alive. No one will. I'll be back shot as soon as they get me out of sight. Attempting escape. I'll never reach no jail."

"You'll reach jail," said the skinny sheriff. "To hang."

"Hang?" said Crezavent. "What am I supposed to have did?"

"Murdered a ranch foreman named McIntosh one night playing a game of high-card alone with him behind a barn by lantern, and taking him out on the prairie and interring him."

"Alone?" said Crezavent. "Then what makes 'em think it was me?"

"You was seen coming and going," said the sheriff.

Then, after an instant's hesitation, after his eyes had flicked over Fane and Arapaho from boot tips to hat crowns, he said, "You other two boys — whoever you are, I don't seem to have nothing for you at the moment but a word or two of precious advice. It's from the little blue-backed reader I used in the fourth grade."

Then without finishing, the sheriff turned and departed with Crezavent. None of the others had even spoken.

When they had gone, Arapaho said, "Well, there you are. All trumped up, of course."

"Why just Crezavent and not you, too?" asked Fane. "And how did they know just where to take him?"

"That was Sheriff Sandy Sanderson," said Arapaho. "He has his ways of knowing."

"But why not you, too?"

"Different sheriffs find themselves presented with different problems."

Flatly then, Arapaho said, "We'll wait about an hour, and then get to it."

"To what?" asked Fane.

"To go in and try to jailbreak him."

"Jailbreak him?" said Fane. "You'd have about one chance in a thousand."

"I know, but we've got to try."

Shocked, Fane said, "He wouldn't do it for either of us!"

"That's where you're wrong," said Arapaho. "You're traveling with a breed of cats, friend. He'd sure as hell do as much for us, even for you. Maybe not a particle more, but as much. So let's get our breath back, and wait a bit, and then move in and play it by ear."

"Not me," said Fane. "Like you just said, I don't happen to belong to that breed of cats."

Arapaho was careful not to look at him.

Fane said, "I was in this to help Bruce Baldecker. I'll not move in any way against constituted authority."

Arapaho, showing no scorn, showing only deep understanding, said, "Well, at least shake hands with me and say goodbye. Men are like anything else. You've got to take them as they come. You take me as I come, and I'll take you as you come. Good enough?"

"You're going in alone?" asked Fane.

"I've told you I have to."

"Then save the handshake," said Fane. "I'm going in with you."

Arapaho seemed unimpressed, one way or the other. He merely nodded.

"What county are we in?" asked Fane.

27

"Messer County."

"What's its county seat?" asked Fane. "I mean what town are we headed for?"

"Polton."

Polton! The town to stay away from.

As Fane sat on the white glazed iron-pipe bed, checking — needlessly, he thought, but at Arapaho's stern order — the heavy S.&M. .44 with its extra weight of lead and extra measure of powder in each of its cartridges, the smashing weapon he had long ago learned to love above all other guns, he could feel the broken springs beneath him, punching up at him into his work pants. The window of the stark grubby little hotel room looked out on a tin roof, painted with sickly blue wagon paint as a rust preventative and as hot even to the eye as a stove lid under the hammering of the zenith sun.

The window was open and the air that came in was as hot as the air that went out, but with minor differences in its composition — the air that came in was sultry with putrid manure and backhouses and noon cooking, greens and beans and bacon fat from somewhere, and the air that went out, bursting across the roof from its imprisonment, was sour with rat droppings and old socks and the acid of assorted grime. Beyond the window and roof, across the street, was a gap-toothed row of one and two story fronts bearing the customary county seat, pioneer trading center signs, in peeling paint. *General Supplies. Mother's Eatery.*

Beer — Whiskey — Fine Liquors. Rugs, Wallpaper, Caskets, Lamps, Elegant Boston Hearse for Hire.

Arapaho, at whose insistence they had registered here, saying that public display at this moment might be a good thing, and that friction that looked you up was sometimes better than the friction you had to look up yourself, and saying, too, that they should have an open harmless looking location while they sized things up, sat relaxed and apparently not bothered or unhappy sipping a bottle of uniced, summer hot beer, finishing every sip as though they were deciding the grave problem of whether to toss the bottle out the window or not.

The roof outside the window was just that, all right, a plain tin roof, but it had seemingly been used by some hotel guests on occasion, frantic by their boxed-in rooms, as a sort of second-floor veranda, for just outside this window was a broken rocking chair, and just to the window's left, barely showing, was the corner of a mussed-up quilt, which had been used as an outdoor pallet.

It was from this corner of the window the man appeared, close to the outside of the wall of the hotel, close to the window sill — peering.

Arapaho at the moment was squinting with disgust down into the neck of his warm bottle of beer. He was half-turned from the window and the man.

To Fane, sitting there, facing the man, he at first seemed like merely a dirty townsman with a touch of idiocy in his face, the hotel handyman perhaps, maybe just fiddling around cleaning up the litter on the veranda.

Fane was halfway through the process of cleaning his gun. At that instant, it was limp on his knee, its hammer at full cock, back, its hammerspur under the ball of his thumb.

He shot the man.

Shot him just once, to kill. Kill instantly. Upward. At where the bone of his nasal bridge joined the bone of the forehead, putting the lead in as neatly and accurately as though he had spent a whole day laying off the target with calipers.

For the man was carrying a sawed-off shotgun, so newly sawed off that its muzzle still showed the hacksaw cut, the metal of its barrel-ends sparkling in the noonday sun like a pair of tin-rimmed spectacles.

The next hour was a mighty, mighty busy one.

Things happened which were expected, things which weren't expected.

The name of the late and so suddenly deceased, as well as anyone could tell, was Jarrett. When you came right down to it, no one knew much about him — except that he'd sent off a telegram at the station under that name. Ordinarily, a gun death was nothing but a gun death, but in this case the victim had been lugging a sawed-off shotgun, a point of disapproval in this rifle and bowie knife county.

Sheriff Sandy Sanderson, the same skinny officer whom Fane had encountered earlier in the day at

Crezavent's arrest, appeared with his same retinue of deputies, asked a few casual questions and left.

He didn't put it in so many words, but his general attitude was that if a man came at you with a shotgun, no matter who you were, no matter how low you were, the only thing to do was to take care of it.

This in fact, seemed to be the attitude of all of Polton.

There appeared one dissenting voice, however. A lone cowboy called the Whistling Kid had spent a little time around the watering-trough constructing, presenting, and hotly debating a theory that this Jarrett, whoever he was, had been on a sort of commercial mission to *sell* the weapon.

"Over the roof?" someone asked him.

"Nobody buys a sawed-off shotgun too public," the Whistling Kid said.

Then someone else, thinking he had the talker on the run, said, "You mean this Fane just misunderstood, and shot him for the hell of it?" But the debater had refused to be defeated, and replied, "I don't know why he shot him, and it's my guess nobody will ever find out, but this Fane knowed what he was doing because a little earlier, he'd even flashed a roll at *me* — as I was standin' in front of Mother's Eatery sucking my teeth — and tried to buy a sawed-off shotgun from *me*. It was *me* who put him onto this Jarrett."

"Why Jarrett?" they'd asked. He had shrugged and said, "It come to me in a hunch."

When this incident finally got back to Fane, Fane said to Arapaho, "Do you know this Whistling Kid?"

"Never heard of him."

"Why on earth would he say a thing like that?"

"That's reasonable," said Arapaho mildly. "No man likes to lose an argument in public. Why worry? It was a mighty fine try, but it didn't convince anyone."

"But he personated me," said Fane. Down in Iraville, to tag a man personally, by actual name, in public, in almost any connection, was a very touchy and discourteous thing to do.

In a mollifying voice, Arapaho said, "Maybe this Whistling Kid's got glanders, ringbones, and spavins!"

Then, when a distant, innocent look crept into Fane's eyes, Arapaho said, "We're here to get Crezavent out of jail, remember?"

They were on their way to the courthouse now, to chat a little further with Sheriff Sanderson, to get the feel of things, and then to the jail, maybe, to see what was what. The sheriff had showed no hostility to them all along the line and they expected none from him now.

That was the way Arapaho said to do it, and Arapaho was the professional here.

A block south of Main Street was the railroad, which separated Front Street from Senate and these three factors — Front with its shops, and Senate Street flanking it on the far side, with its parlor houses and bucket-of-blood saloons and corrals — was a little specialized Polton of its own, with its own customs and subjects of conversation and deadfall whiskey. The courthouse, through poor anticipation on the part of town planners, had been erected here on the original town plat and now stood without even a court square between a couple of pink-dirt eroded lots, each with mounded earth and a half-dug foundation for an ephemeral business enterprise that came to nothing.

The courthouse itself was a smallish ugly cube, painted slippery white, with rubbish around the ledge of its doorstep and what looked like bird's nests coughing out in places from under its shingles. The row of four windows upstairs, up under the eaves, showed blacksmith-wrought bars, old-looking at one end and frowsy lace curtains and potted plants at the other. The bars, Fane was sure, were not for the sheriff and his family; the lace curtains were not for the prisoners.

As Fane and Arapaho approached the building up the short walk, two men appeared from within the courthouse and stood for a moment in the sunlight on the front step. Fane and Arapaho, each equally amazed, joined them.

One was Crezavent, free of handcuffs, wearing his gun. He was doing something unusual — he was smiling. And smiling sociably. Smiling and beaming and patting another man, smiling himself, on the shoulder.

The other man wore serviceable batwing chaps, and was short and chunky, compressed looking. Even his face. He looked like the muscle was all there, all right, but it had been hammered down until he was as powerful as a locomotive piston.

He had a roll of big green banknotes in his hand, a roll about the size of a bartender's fist, and as they came up he was peeling off a few. He peeled off five one hundreds, and handed them to Crezavent.

"So you're not going to sue Mr. Southworth, or the sheriff, or me, or nobody else for false arrest? And you're satisfied with this as a settlement? Complete and in full?"

"Complete and in full," said Crezavent, ramming the money in the breast pocket of his shirt. "Anybody can make a mistake."

Now Arapaho spoke. "Beautiful day."

Crezavent and the money-giver seemed to notice Fane and Arapaho for the first time. Crezavent said, "Mr. McIntosh, these are a couple o' my dear friends." He mentioned no names.

"Glad to meet you," said McIntosh, careful not to survey them.

He looked at his watch. "Well, I'd better be getting the grocery supplies, and rollin' back to the place."

When he had gone, Crezavent said, "That was McIntosh, the man I was supposed to have kilt."

"I got that idea," said Arapaho.

"And all the time he was out in a line camp, alone, laying out wolf poison."

"A foreman?" said Fane. "And not even bothering to tell his boss."

"He must be independent," said Arapaho.

"Yes," said Crezavent heartily. "That's the very word to describe him — independent."

Now the money came out of Crezavent's pocket again. He thumbed three one hundreds from the wad, handed one to Fane, two to Arapaho, and kept the other two for himself.

Fane, shying back, refused his. He said, "What's this for? I wasn't falsely arrested."

"Yo're one of us, ain't you?" said Crezavent. "And you had the food that got me far enough to be false arrested, didn't you?"

Arapaho said coldly, "You've hired on for another job."

"Not me," said Crezavent. "Not exactly."

"I told you," said Arapaho, "that I wanted no more work at this time north of the Platte."

"What's happening here, what are you all talking about?" asked Fane.

"That's what I'd like to know," said Arapaho, and his voice was like sandpaper.

"They heard we weren't being needed no longer up north at Split Butte," said Crezavent. "So they stopped us on our way back and took us on. That all there is to it."

"You mean the sheriff was in on it?" asked Arapaho.

"No, they just wanted a few words with me and knowed that would bring you into town after me. The sheriff wasn't in on it. They just hoodwinked him a little."

"What is this job?" asked Arapaho furiously.

"It's no job at all really," said Crezavent. "They just want us to show a few guns around town for a few days, on their side."

"I want none of it, not a particle," said Fane.

"You don't have no choice now," said Crezavent. "You stood by while I took their money."

"That part of it is the truth," warned Arapaho. "Don't try to run out. It just wouldn't work. I'll talk us out."

CHAPTER
FOUR

No one seemed to have anything further to say. They turned abruptly from Senate, crossed the Senate Street roadway, stepped over the railroad tracks, crossed the Front Street roadway, and mounted the three wooden steps to Front. Up on the boardwalk here, Arapaho said to Crezavent, "This way. We took a room. We're staying at a flicker nest called the Polton House, where you can take a bath."

"I take my baths as I take pretzels with my beer: when, if, and as I so desire," said Crezavent.

Arapaho, bringing him up to date on events, told him about the man Jarrett, Fane had shot on the roof.

"He was first on our list," said Crezavent, sounding pleased. "He was brought in to take out Mr. Southworth himself. Roof, eh? They tell me he was knowed for never giving a man an even break. Matter of fact, I was offered fifty dollars, special, myself, private, to handle him."

"It happened an hour ago," said Fane. "You mean to tell me the word hadn't got to you, even in jail?"

"Oh, sure. But just the Jarrett part, which was wrong, of course. His real name was Brynfield. I made him from Arapaho's description of him. In fact, before

Arapaho come along, I used to travel with him." With a great pretense of generosity, he said, "Fifty dollars, Mr. Fane. You'll have twenty-five dollars coming from me. When I get paid, I'm going to split it with you for your assistance."

"I want no part of it," said Fane curtly.

"When you speak to me," said Crezavent serenely, "speak in an agreeable voice or not at all."

"He's never been paid for killing a man before," said Arapaho, again stepping in and smoothing things out.

"Well, there's always a first time," said Crezavent, following it through, but momentarily confused by this extraordinary item of information.

Now, as Fane walked along beside them in silence, he knew one thing for certain, for an absolute fact. Despite Arapaho's warning to the contrary, he'd run out, and now. He had no doubt he could do it, do the actual getting away part; he had trailed hostile Indians, and had them trail him and in escape and attack on the prairies knew most of the lessons in the book like a fox. He could get from Polton to Iraville without a soul coming up close enough behind him to gunsight him, but after he'd reached Iraville, what?

Iraville and Betty. One thing he knew in his heart of hearts: A man like Crezavent treasured slights and affronts, hoarded them up, saved them, and eventually satisfied them in savage rapture.

He could go home to Iraville, of course, and pack their two deer hide trunks, and sneak off.

Or he could kill Crezavent. Here. Now. This minute. And get it done with.

With a chill, he realized those were the two choices, and the only two.

Now the sun, which had so many times punished Fane, this time saved his life.

This was one of the more thickly built-up sections of Front Street. All at once there it was, a few yards in front of them on the boardwalk as they strode along, and Fane seemed to be the only one of them that noticed it, the giant soot-gray frog.

Distorted, squat, monstrous, there it lay in their path, the shadow, as though tissue-paper thin it were plastered to the scuffed planking of yellow pine.

Just a shadow. A shadow with apparently nothing to make it.

By Fane's idly swinging gun hand was the window of a saddle shop and next to it an alley of packed dirt, and beyond the alley mouth, set in the walk, dirt here, the big squared timbers of a flush-level feed and grain scale.

As Fane's hand swung up to his gun, he slipped it fluidly from its leather — and shot the man who came lunging out of the alley mouth, weapon at full cock.

Shot him with his heavy S. & W., almost close enough to count the stitches around his breast pocket, and slammed him into tangled knees and elbows, dead.

A crowd gathered, and one of the first, to Fane's secret respect, was Sheriff Sandy Sanderson. When the sheriff examined the body, and turned and appraised the onlookers, one by one, he did it with the casual but white-hot concentration that seizes a woman when she threads a needle. Now, for the first time, Fane knew here was a real sheriff. Forget the shell of political polish, refuse to be misdirected by it, and you had a real law officer.

"Anybody know his real name?" asked the sheriff.

"A Texas man, he claimed," said someone. "Name of the Whistling Kid."

"If you call a milk-cow Bossy, that's her name," said the sheriff patiently. "And if you call a bronco Two Spot, foolish as it sounds to the bronco, that's his or her name. But don't stand there and tell me no man is named the Whistling Kid. No loving mother would fasten it on to her adored infant and no preacher would baptise and christen it thus. Now, anybody want to try again? I asked for his *real* name."

Nobody wanted to try again.

"Take him away," said the sheriff, in much the tone he would have referred to a load of rubbish.

When the assembly had dispersed and Arapaho and Crezavent and Fane were on their way again to the hotel, the law completely satisfied at the result of the ambush that backfired, Crezavent was the first of them to speak.

In a voice that was heavy with hate and envy, he said, "Arapaho, you wouldn't be running some kind of a double game on me, would you?"

"No, I wouldn't," said Arapaho. "Never. What do you mean?"

"You wouldn't be bringing in a stranger, figuring to get rid of me somehow, figuring to have him take my place with you?"

"Of course" said Arapaho. "What gave you that idea?"

40

"Let's put it this way," said Crezavent. "For a man like this Mr. Fane here, who is such a poor draw and all that, he sure beats two mighty fast guns, you and me, to it. And beats us every time."

"Accidents, both of them," said Arapaho.

"That's right," said Fane. "These are the first two men I've ever killed since I was a boy." Even Arapaho gaped a little at this one.

"Since you was a boy?" said Crezavent.

"And it wasn't a man. It was another boy," said Fane. Trying to belittle it further, trying to make it seem nothing, trying to ease the situation, he added, "And then I only shot him in the back."

"Now there's childhood play for you," said Crezavent. "Little boys shooting other little boys in the back."

"This boy was a teenager, a drunken Sioux being looked for by six detachments of cavalry. He was chasing my mother through our cabbage patch down by the creek. I heard my mother yell but was too far away to get to them. I shot him with my father's rifle from up on the roof of our cabin."

The men, each of them, looked deeply moved.

But the mood of sympathy in Crezavent came and went in a flick, and by the time they were all of them seated, boots off, in the hotel room, he was the same old Crezavent again, nothing but animal body and animal mind. "I'm hungry," he said. "And I ain't never eat nothing in this burg except behind bars."

"Food in good time," said Arapaho. "But first I got to know about this list you mentioned — the one Jarrett was on."

"Well," said Crezavent. "The Whistling Kid was on it, too, for that matter. Is that what yo're hinting at? But he was lumped with the others. If you think Fane's got something due for that one, too, he ain't. That was just part of our work."

Fane had a little spasm in his face, he thought he was going to retch. It wasn't just the killing, it was everything, and mainly it was the hideous situation he had brought upon Betty through being a mule-headed brute. It was a sort of a tic, and he felt it, and tried to hide it with his hand but they saw it, each of them.

"You want to throw up, don't you?" said Arapaho.

"Yes, you do," said Crezavent, inspecting him almost medically. "And some of the best killers that ever lived get took that way afterward. I knowed one over in Idaho that cried like a baby. *Afterward*. Folks thought it was remorse, but once he told me what it was. He was still mad at the corpse. He'd got himself all worked up and now he was sorry he couldn't do it again. Just keep on doing it. I have a feeling this gent, Mr. Fane, has a similar trouble."

"What kind of a mess have you got us into?" asked Arapaho.

"It's one of these that comes and goes, like a shuffle of cards, everywhere, all the time, nothing to it, really. There's this man, Southworth, that has a ranch aways east o' here. He had a little spare cash to invest and it must have come to him in a bad dream to own a part of this big city and he bought a part interest of the hellhole, here and there. Certain parties say he tricked 'em, and don't want him around, and say stay out and stick to cows."

"Just a partnership dispute?" said Arahapo incredulously.

"That just about sums it up," said Crezavent carelessly.

"For partnership disputes there are courts," said Arapaho. "You don't bring in gunthrowers like Crezavent and me and this Jarrett and the Whistling Kid."

"Tempers run high someplaces," said Crezavent smugly.

Arapaho said, "So this Mr. Southworth brought us in, and sent McIntosh around to the jail to get you out again, and pay you. And this McIntosh mentioned a few names. And that's all you can tell?"

"That's about all there is to tell, that I can think of now," said Crezavent. "Why the cross-examination? We've hired out on a heap less, and you know it."

To Fane, Arapaho said, "Is it your fond hope to stay reasonably alive?"

"I'd have no objection to it, I can tell you that," said Fane.

"Then we'll just look into this a little," said Arapaho.

"You mean I'm running a little deal of my own on the side?" said Crezavent but showing no anger.

"I didn't say that," said Arapaho. "But it's been tried before."

"I guess it has at that," said Crezavent, amused. "But whatever you find, if anything, don't pull out on me. We've already took their money, remember."

The inside of Mother's Eatery, long and bare and narrow, had once been a storeroom, and was simply that and nothing more now, when you came right down to it. Board floors, board walls, and board ceiling, with uncovered yellow pine tables. The tables, too, remained bare until a customer sat at one — then bone-handled eating implements, bent tin plates, and a loaf of bread, sliced, on end, like a stack of heaven, appeared. Appeared silently, for "Mother" herself, if she had ever existed, had long ago dematerialized and was now replaced by the typical, customary Chinese owner. And if you could just close your eyes while you ate, you had to admit the food was food all right, and not too bad. His unpronounceable Chinese name meant "Tigerblood Warrior." No one, even liquor happy, called him Mother.

Arapaho sat them at a table in the center of the room for, as Crezavent had recently said, much of a gunman's value to his employer was public display.

And everyone certainly looked at them; they were notorious already. Fane, of the three of them, was the only one who showed any nervousness.

Another thing — Fane seemed to be the main one people were interested in. Those two deaths had made him famous.

Arapaho said to Crezavent, "You know, I can't seem to get this straight. This list, and people taking potshots at us. Tell me a little more about the list." His voice was almost inaudible.

"Like I said before," said Crezavent, also in a whisper, "it wasn't a list really, it was, you might say, just general discussion. And this is no place to hash it over."

Tigerblood Warrior was at the table's edge and Arapaho said, "Steak!"

The steaks, when they showed up, appeared on a platter about the size of barrel-end and were country style, sliced very thin, heavily floured, heavily salt-and-peppered, touched up mystically with garlic, by and large a strange flavor here. In tureens and bowls and smaller platters all around it were green beans and bacon, mountains of mashed potatoes and butter, and creamed onions. They really worked on it.

When they had finished, and sighed in delirium, Arapaho got back to business.

He said, "What got into you, Crezavent, taking on a thing like this blind?"

"I'll tell you what got into me," said Crezavent. "Money and jail bars."

"We don't stand a chance in hell," said Arapaho. "And by that I mean a chance in hell of even staying alive. If we don't learn a heap more about this, and learn it fast."

This was a different Arapaho. It was the man, Fane realized, who really ran the team, who gave the orders.

"Now here's the thing for us to do," he said. "To start with — and I mean now — Crezavent, you go back to that alley the Whistling Kid jumped out of. See where it comes from, what's behind it, I mean. But most important, ask a few questions here and there. Did anybody see him? With anybody else? If so, with who?"

"That sounds pretty silly to me," said Crezavent. "Who cares where the alley feeds back into? And what if he was seen with somebody?"

"Then, if you don't care to do it," said Arapaho, "just say so. Go back to that saloon we passed, The Stockman's Rest, and order yourself a cool fishbowl beer and let me and Mr. Fane handle it. But don't never call me silly."

"I'll do it," said Crezavent. "What are you and him going to do?"

"Mr. Fane is going back to the jail, pretending to offer bail, and pretending to be surprised to hear you're out. And picking up what he can from the law itself about McIntosh and Mr. Southworth when this fact comes out in the conversation."

"And you?" asked Crezavent.

"Me? I'm not just certain at the moment. These businesses Mr. Southworth bought himself into — the ones they seem to be trying to get him out of — I can't recall just what you said they were?"

"One of them was a shoe shop, I think," said Crezavent, getting to his feet. "I'll see you later. At The Stockman's Rest?"

"Stockman's Rest it is," agreed Arapaho.

They waited a minute after he had gone, then went out onto the street. Arapaho, almost sullenly thoughtful, remained silent.

Fane said, "Any special questions you want me to ask the sheriff about this McIntosh and Southworth?"

And suddenly he realized that, boxed in by his remark, he had for the first time declared himself in the game.

"You're not going to the jail," said Arapaho. "I want you to come with me."

"Then why lie to Crezavent?"

"Crezavent's happier, and works better when he doesn't know everything."

"Where are we going?"

"To the railroad station."

"Now that's the first sensible thing I've heard so far," said Fane, grinning. "To catch a train to Paris, France, I hope."

"You'll see," said Arapaho.

CHAPTER
FIVE

They walked down the station platform and into the building, a little green painted structure with a big sign above its door: *POLTON*.

The stationmaster, a feeble looking man with parched skin and dry, pouched eye sockets, sat on a stool at a telegraph instrument behind a counter. "He looks like he might be a hard man to fool," said Arapaho. "But we'll see."

The elderly stationmaster, who was at the moment receiving on his instrument, finished his incoming message, got up and walked over to them. Sociably. Obviously a lonesome man.

He arched his eyebrows expectantly, politely. Then, in an immediate follow up, his visage changed slightly, but only slightly, and he said, "Now I recognize you." He pointed with interest and admiration at Fane. "You're the quick-draw artist that outshot that man with his twelve gauger."

"That's right," said Arapaho, putting a heavy overlay of admiration in his voice, too. For reputation, for future business purposes, Fane decided.

"Yeah," said Arapaho dolorously. "Sad, wasn't it?"

"I wouldn't call it sad," said the stationmaster. "He was all set to kill Mr. Fane, wasn't he?"

"Kill both of us, I expect," said Arapaho. "But no matter what way you look at it, no man likes to kill his brother-in-law."

Stunned by this choice item of gossip for Main Street, the stationmaster said hoarsely, "You mean this Jarrett was Mr. Fane's brother-in-law?"

"Once was," said Arapaho, "before he turned bad and left the family hearth and home and took up with dregs and worse. That was a long, long time ago, before he growed that long jaw and when his eyes was blue instead of brown."

The stationmaster said, "You sure you got the right man in mind? I never heard of a growed man sprouting a long jaw and having his eyes change color."

"A life o' crime does strange things," said Arapaho.

Fane, not knowing Arapaho's goal, simply remained mute.

"The way he nailed him down finally, and without doubt," said Arapaho, "was by that broke little finger of his, shaped like a baby sweet potato."

"That could have been just an interesting coincidence," said the stationmaster, desiring to prolong such a noteworthy and sociable conversation. "I'm sure many a man has a broken little finger shaped like a sweet potato —"

"That was Mr. Fane's contention at first," said Arapaho. "But after I'd talked to him a bit, and after he'd studied it over, he decided it was his brother-in-law, all right. And you mixed it up a little, too, when you put out the wrong name."

"Me?" said the stationmaster, startled. "Wrong?"

"I talked to him about that, too," said Arapaho. "And explained anyone, even a stationmaster, even a telegrapher, could make a mistake."

"A railroad telegrapher!" said the stationmaster. "If a railroad telegrapher made mistakes, he could pile up a mess of cars!"

"It was a natural mistake," said Arapaho, seeming to try to mollify him.

They looked at each other, stiff-faced.

Finally, a little dry-voiced, the stationmaster asked, "What was this mistake?"

"After you wrote it down, you couldn't read your own writing," said Arapaho. "You said the name was Jarrett, but it was Jarnette. You went and scribbled 'n' as a double 'r' likely, and left off the final 'e'."

"Not me," said the stationmaster decisively. "I write a mighty plain, real oldfashioned copperplate."

He went to a sheaf of flimsies on a wire hook, riffled through them, at last located one he had been searching for, and brought it forward. Glancing at it intently, he said, "Yep. Just like I claimed. Jarrett it is."

He gave it a triumphant flip, and started to return to the hook with it.

"Naturally, we don't get to see it," said Arapaho courteously.

"All telegrams is confidential," said the stationmaster, halting.

50

"That's understandable," said Arapaho. "Mr. Fane, I'm sure, realizes that. His brother-in-law is confidential, too. Well, you've proved it to us, or at least to yourself, so we thank you. Let's go, Mr. Fane. We're wasting our time here."

Angered, the stationmaster held up the telegram face outward, for the briefest of instants, said, "See? Jarrett!" and walked away.

Arapaho, who seemed hardly to flick his sight in its direction, said apologetically, "He's right, Mr. Fane. Jarrett it is. He's right and I'm wrong."

"Make the two of you feel better?" asked the stationmaster as they departed.

"A heap better," said Arapaho.

Outside on the platform, Fane said, "Don't tell me, in nothing flat, twelve feet away, you read that telegram."

"If you've ever been in Apache country, as I've been, and you see a patch of mesquite on the hillside, you look at it, and you look at it with everything you've got, and you don't take the day doing it — for it better be the same down to the last twig the next time you look at it."

"Was the telegram important?" asked Fane. "What did it say?"

"In the first place, our stationmaster *did* make a mistake. Or at least his story got bungled being told over and over again. Jarrett didn't send that telegram, he received it."

When Fane merely waited, Arapaho continued. "It was sent from a sagebrush railroad shack about a quarter of a mile west of Grissle's hut, from a place just knowed as 'Nineteen.' It read: *Tell Fred Crezavent has took Southworth's offer said as much when I made him your proposal up at Split Butte which affair has blew up to nothing. Stop. McIntosh was here before me. Stop. Grissle says a new man has joined them and the three of them from the sign they left were heading south toward Polton. Stop. Grissle knows nothing about this new man. Stop. I did the best I could and am coming home. (signed) Lyman.*"

"So Crezavent had already contracted you," said Fane. "With McIntosh up there at Split Butte."

"It appears so," said Arapaho, sounding just a little bleak.

"Without saying anything about it to you."

"He knows that after the Split Butte thing I intended nothing more for the time being north of the Platte."

"And arranged the whole business on it. McIntosh maybe to tip off the sheriff to stop us."

"It looks that way."

"To suck you into this Polton thing where you wanted in or not."

Arapaho said, "It worked, didn't it?"

"What kind of man is this Crezavent?" said Fane, looking fiery.

"That kind of a man," said Arapaho dryly. "And a man that can show a gun quicker than most men can show a fist."

The Stockman's Rest, when they came into it, proved to be a big fancy place glowing in sticky mahogany varnish, dazzling in opalescent pyramided

52

goblets, and softly lighted with lamps and frosted glass shades, everything whispering money, money, money. The room was not packed, but what customers were there gave off an aroma of affluence. Crezavent was not in sight.

Arapaho, spurs clinking, strode to the bar and Fane followed him. The bar, too, was almost void of customers but there were two men behind it, a sneaky-looking barman and a portly, overdressed man beside him.

This second man had the till open and was checking the cash, going through the silver and banknotes in the drawer with unbelievable speed. He had a pouting, florid face, spangled with a snarl of red threadlike veins, obviously recently massaged, and he exuded talc and pomade; only the black bone tip of a cross-drawn gun butt peeped from the left-hand side of his open coat.

Any man that went in for a cross-draw, Fane reflected, was, to say the least, a little heavy on the gun-conscious side. It was no proof at all that he was an eye-popping gun artist, but it showed he gave his weapon a trifle more than due thought.

Arapaho said, "I was supposed to meet —"

He got no further when the barman said, "He was here and left. Told me to send you down the next block to the Eclipse. And frankly I was glad to get rid of him. Tried everything to start a fuss with me. Said they was a fly cooked inside the rye bread of his free lunch sandwich."

"That's him, all right," said Arapaho, nodding. "Thank you for your courtesy in not having trouble with him. Man, would he have looked foolish if you'd have shook your fist in his face, or slapped him on the jaw, or something."

While this was going on, the second man, the pink-faced, pomaded man, registered complete detachment.

Fane, to his surprise at his growing personal involvement, felt a desire to know a little about him.

To this man, Fane said, "Excuse me, sir. And please don't take offense. It's not in any way meant as such. But didn't I see you once on the stage in Chicago? As I remember it, you were playing what I think they call the lead role in a wonderful drama called *The Most Handsome Man in the World*."

The pink-faced man stopped counting and looked up. His face was beatific under the flagrant flattery. "It couldn't have been me, friend. It must have been one of those doubles some men have that you hear about. I'm Fred Freneau. I own this place."

Now Fane on impulse, on a little more than impulse really, because he remembered that name Fred on Jarrett's telegram, and because this man was so borderline and could so easily fit into any picture between respectability and nonrespectability, said, "Is this one of the places you and Mr. Southworth own in partnership?"

Arapaho turned toward Fane and stared at him.

The cordiality blew from Fred Freneau like mist before a chill breeze.

He said half aloud, fingering the money in the drawer, "Fifty-four, sixty-one, sixty-six — sorry, you made me lose count. I do not discuss my personal affairs, sir. Sixty-six, eighty-six —"

"Let's go," said Arapaho.

They went.

Out in the sunlight, on the boardwalk, Fane said, "The Stockman's Rest. That's one of them they're quarreling over, all right. I'd bet on it."

"Yes," agreed Arapaho. "I think so, too. And I'll tell you something else. To sign a partnership with that Fred Freneau, our Mr. Southworth must be really yokel."

"Now we've got our Fred, I'm pretty sure," said Fane. "I wonder who the Lyman in the telegram is?"

"Is, or was," said Arapaho. "It could have been the Whistling Kid."

"I doubt it," said Fane. "The Whistling Kid would have been here in Polton at the moment, I'd say, like Jarrett."

"I'd say so, too, on second thought," said Arapaho. "Lyman would be somebody, some next to nobody, probably, someone who takes Freneau's money when Freneau needs him. He needed us this time to go up in the Split Butte country and try to recruit us away from Mr. Bruce Baldecker down here to Mr. Fred Freneau."

In a few minutes, they had their supposition proved to them, and they knew it for a fact, for black letters on a sign over a door said: Eclipse Saloon, Freneau and Southworth, Proprietors.

CHAPTER
SIX

The door set level with the ground without a doorstep, was small, but when they were inside, Fane thought that was all a funnel needed, too, a little opening at one end; inside, the room, smoke streamered, was jam-packed with boisterous, sweating humanity. It wasn't too small a place either, with makeshift plastered walls, the plaster so thin you could easily see the lath impressions beneath it, decorated with lithographs of hurdy-gurdy girls and harness racehorses.

The hard-looking customers at the bar, knee-booted most of them and rank-smelling, were as thick as buzzards clotting a month dead cow. Though on a small scale, other enticements than drink were offered, and the place must be a gold mine. To the rear, through an open door, could be seen a table encircled with cowboys and wagoners, before them on the tabletop big whiskey glasses, scarcely holding a thimbleful when you came right down to it, all glass, greasy broken cards, money, and cheap personal items of jewelry. To the left, through an arched doorway thinly curtained, with a curtain made up of red and blue and green glass beads and fingerlengths of bamboo, could be seen a steep flight of stairs leading up, Fane was sure, to rooms and girls. A few girls were in sight down here, too; circulating like water bugs in a stagnant rain barrel.

They saw Crezavent. He was tottering a little unsteadily, a beer mug held to his chin, looking helplessly intoxicated.

"He should be sitting down instead of standing up," said Fane.

"That means he's out for a fuss," said Arapaho. "Many a hasty man, on the lookout for a little bit of advantage, has been fooled by it."

They went up to him.

He said, "Well, I went back into that alley, like you said to, Arapaho."

"What happened?" asked Arapaho, pretending great interest.

"Nothing," said Crezavent. "Just what I so expected — nothing."

"Drink down your beer," said Arapaho. "We've decided to take a little ride."

Crezavent set his beer down, unfinished, now all business. "Where to?" he asked.

"Mr. Southworth's ranch," said Arapaho. "If you know offhand where it is."

"I've heard," said Crezavent. "But as I've been tryin' to get across to you, any business we have with Southworth goes through his foreman, McIntosh. Do you get it. Not Southworth, but through McIntosh to Southworth."

"You do it your way, I'll do it my way," said Arapaho.

They got their horses from the Good Luck Livery Stable, and soon they were out of town, heading east.

For a while it was the sort of land Fane was so familiar with, the great plain rolling, the swells of rich grassland, the occasional eczema of splotchy greasewood, the shallow bowls of sage, all speckled with cows, to the luminous blue horizon with its chains of snowy flat-bottomed clouds, a paradise to the eye as great as any westerner could possibly dream of. Thin lines of alders crisscrossed the flatlands, signifying the presence of sweet water streams.

As they rode along, Crezavent told them of his experience in the alley.

"I done exactly like you said, Arapaho. Along the alley, mainly, is back doors to shops and offices and such. Ask a few questions, you said, and I did, whenever I see anyone, which was seldom, and no one even knowed what I was talking about. It was a complete waste of time and almost got me bad burnt besides."

"Burnt?" said Arapaho. "How is that?"

"About halfway down the alley, about midway between Front and Main, they was this sorry-looking blacksmith shop, in a kind of vacant lot. Its two big front doors was swung wide open. Inside, was a nice lookin' bay, tied. It had on a set of shoes that looked almost new to me."

Crezavent, unused to lengthy conversation, took a shallow breath and continued. "The smith, a hoop-legged little hard-case feller, a scarred up ex-cowboy if I ever see one, took off the bay's shoes and tossed 'em in a corner. A-one condition. That bay didn't need no new shoes. Well, naturally curious, I stood around and waited.

"He had a horseshoe blank in the forge already cherry-red hot. As he picked it up with his tongs and was carryin' it to his anvil, I asked him about had he seen the Whistling Kid come by. He said no, and then this thing happened. As he passed me he sort of swung the tongs and the red-hot blank swished about a quarter of an inch from my hand, my gun hand, by the way, which was hooked onto my belt. It touched my holster."

He exhibited a black, bubbly looking mark on the holster leather. "Like a rabbit I jumped back, but it was close."

"So you shot him, of course," said Fane.

"Why should I?" said Crezavent, surprised. "It was a accident pure and simple, and accidents will happen."

"Give me your opinion of the whole thing," said Arapaho.

"I don't have no opinion," said Crezavent. "There's nothing to have no opinion about; it was all just like I said."

A little later, Crezavent, restless with their company, rode on a short distance ahead of them.

Arapaho said, "You know, of course. Crezavent was looking at the Whistling Kid's horse when he was looking at that bay. The Kid was having its shoes changed because he'd been in trouble somewhere else and its tracks were known. And the smith knew it. He had to know it. Take new shoes off, put new, but different, shoes on! This was, to say the least, a man friendly to them. You know what I think?"

"What?" asked Fane.

"The smith must have knowed — the whole town knowed by then — that the Whistling Kid had gone to a better world. He went right on with the job, though. Because he'd been ordered to. And because, if things went right, well maybe the nag would get forgotten in the excitement and he'd have himself a horse for free."

"You mean if he was friendly to them, he tried to shoot Crezavent on purpose?"

"What do you think?"

A little after, when Crezavent had joined them again, Arapaho said, "Did it come out in the conversation with him what this blacksmith's name was?"

"Not with me," said Crezavent. "But his name was Jones. A little boy walking down the alley blowing an elm bark whistle yelled, 'Hullo, Jonesy' at him."

"Could be a nickname or something," Arapaho said.

"The name is Jones, all right," said Crezavent, beginning to get hostile because he had been contradicted. "That's what the sign over the door said: Lyman Jones, Blacksmith, Tinware Mended, Scythes ReTempered & ReGround."

"Lyman," said Arapaho.

"Lyman and Fred," said Fane.

But Crezavent was off and away from them again, dancing his mount in little nervous circles.

They, each of them in his own way, sized up Southworth's place as they rode up to it. Here lived the man for whom they would kill or get killed.

In this country everything outside a town's limits (unless maybe it was a homesteader's farm) was a ranch, whether it was a shack with one cow about to calve, or a cumbersome Eastern-style mansion with a corner turret, shingled, and gingerbread cornices and more land and cows than a sixth grade arithmetic could total.

Mr. Southworth, whose brand they were later to learn was the Box S, was one of those in-between, one of the hardly noticeable average.

The railroads, which, like a thunderclap, had taken cows out and brought money in, in such enormity, had, too, brought back a flurry of Eastern fashions and manners and high-toned fads, flouted in a few instances by some new rich wives, and even, in some instances by the ranchers themselves. But this hoity-toity sickness had touched very few. Apparently the Southworths looked with contempt on these newfangled veneers.

The ranch buildings were solid respectable with no show of either opulence or frugality. The barns and sheds were in good order, weathered, but not too weathered; the windmill was an expensive piece of equipment, a little rusty but not too rusty; the ranch workshop small but okay. The first thing they all looked at, of course, was the bunkhouse, which was nice and large, and the cookhouse.

You couldn't tell the wealth of an outfit, ever, by its ranch house, its residence, but you could estimate the size of its working crew, few or many, by its bunkhouse, and this bunkhouse was big, with a cookhouse to match.

They knew without saying so to each other that this was a thriving outfit, that their boss was, in all probability, a rich man — and understood, for one thing, how he had got together sufficient capital to buy into those Polton businesses with Fred Freneau.

The buildings were built on a sort of ragged circle about a carefully watered and tended disc of grassy lawn, and this, they felt, was not show off but for the boss' personal comfort. Midway, in the center of the far semicircle, the ranch house faced them. It was a story and a half cottage, moss green painted, with a long dormer window above the porch roof and a little spindle and ball moss green railing enclosing the porch itself. On the porch were two humble woven rawhide chairs.

A remarkable scene was being enacted on the ground in front of the porch step. A middle-aged man in a once fine gray wool suit but worn cowboots had a second man on the ground spread eagled beneath him — a young cowhand with curley golden hair. The man in gray, the one on top, was pallid-faced, full-lipped, and looked as though he was trying to shove a pint whiskey bottle neck into the cowhand's ear. The hand was contorting his face and threshing his head away. Finally, however, the gray man succeeded, if only for a brief instant, and out gushed a yellowish liquid.

"All right, now," said the man in gray. "Get up."

They both got up.

"Feel better?" asked the man in gray. "It will," said the man in gray. "Give it time. Take the day off."

The cowhand walked away, miserably.

"Bad earache," said the man in gray. "Poured some hot urine into it. My grandmother's favorite cure. I don't know why he fought it; it was his own urine. I'm Paul Southworth. If you boys are looking for a job, I'm sorry. As you must know, nobody hires at this season."

"You've already hired us," said Arapaho. "I'm Arapaho; this is Mr. Crezavent. And this is Mr. Fane, the gentleman who self-defensed that Jarrett and the Whistling Kid."

"Is that so?" said Southworth noncommittally, but inspecting them carefully and with respect. "I believe I've heard your names, but you've made the trip out here for nothing, whatever your business is. Mr. McIntosh, my foreman, handles certain aspects of my affairs, and Mr. McIntosh is back in Polton at the moment. I'd suggest you go back there, and lay your matter before *him*."

"Oh, no you don't," said Arapaho. "Get down boys." They all dismounted. "We've already taken your money, but I, for one, don't kill a man unless I know why."

Southworth was not at all abashed. He said, "Killing is not my way of doing things. I want you firmly to understand that."

"But the paying for it was," said Arapaho. "You talk straight to me, or you'll regret the day you were born."

The countenances facing Southworth were stony. Even Crezavent, who showed his dislike at the evasion, glared a shadow of that always near-at-hand persecution complex.

"Why did you hire us?" asked Arapaho.

"I'll tell you," said Southworth, completely changing his manner. "The question is fair enough, and I'll tell you. There's a little mix-up, and the sheriff, who is an honest enough man, I guess, simply won't step in and jeopardize his up-coming election. Or at least that's the way I see it. You see, I had this little extra capital, and the idea came to me to invest it in town properties. For Linda. Linda is my daughter. I'm a lonesome widower."

"So you invested it with Fred Freneau," said Arapaho.

"As a matter of fact, I did. Though I must admit you're pretty well posted."

"You went partner in the Eclipse, and The Stockman's Rest." Arapaho kept his voice level. "And what else?"

"A nice big brick domicile on Front, between East and Oak Streets."

"I know the place," said Crezavent. "Ten minutes in town and I heard of it. You don't mean domicile; you mean whorehouse."

"The more customary reference, and I must say the more graceful, is 'social center'," said Southworth.

"Just one more question for the hell of it," said Arapaho. "The Eclipse has girls, gambling, and liquor. Your social center shorely has girls, gambling and liquor, for that, plus a piano, is just about all a social center is. Does The Stockman's Rest have girls and gambling, too, tucked away somewhere out of sight?"

"As a matter of fact, yes," said Southworth. "I'm being honest with you, yes."

"What a nice little bequest of town properties, if bequest is what you meant, for Miss Linda," said Fane.

"And now you come to my point," said Southworth. "I'm no reformer. I've knocked about considerably in my youth, but it's my idea to change those places, clean them up, and put them to entirely different uses. The Eclipse, which is the worst, possibly, I'll make into a little bakery shop, a little bakery shop with iced cookies and such. The house on Front could be converted into a dandy suite of offices for lawyers and so on. The Stockman's Rest would serve nothing but drinks and elegant food, like they do in San Francisco."

"And Fred Freneau says no," said Fane.

"He won't listen to it. The present situation shovels in the money, and money turns his head."

Even Crezavent was interested. He said, "But where are you going to get the customers to fill these mighty high class places?"

"The railroad," said Southworth. "The railroad will bring them in." His eyes got dreamy. "That railroad should have been nailed down its entire length, from east to west, with golden spikes."

"But why us?" pressed Arapaho.

"You see," said Southworth, "we signed one of those perfectly ordinary partnership agreements where if one party dies the business goes automatically, lock, stock, and barrel, to the surviving partner. He's trying to have me killed."

"But hasn't Mr. Fane removed that fear?" asked Arapaho.

"You don't know Fred Freneau," said Southworth. "New men have taken their places, or are already on the way."

A girl came out of the house and stood on the front porch. She was about Betty's age, Fane reflected, with a golden skin, golden hair, and golden eyes, and dressed not as the adored daughter of a wealthy man but in serviceable stiff workclothes, like an overworked housekeeper. The clothes might have been of her own choice, of course, and not, as the ugly thought came and went, her father's choice. She said. "You must excuse me, gentlemen, but my father has tuberculosis, and extended discussions make him ill."

Arapaho taking the lead, they mumbled apologies and left. For awhile, on the way back to Polton, no one spoke.

Then Arapaho said, "He might have told us a true story, but I'm sure there's more to it."

"A man like that Freneau appeared to me," said Fane, "might do exactly as he said."

"I've had more experience with men like Fred Freneau than you have," said Arapaho. "And if he wanted a partner dead, he wouldn't bring in anyone like the Whistling Kid and Jarrett to do it. Not unless something else went wrong first, along the line. He'd kill a partner himself, ambush him maybe, in the dark of the moon along some lonesome road."

CHAPTER
SEVEN

"I don't see why yo're so bothered," said Crezavent. "We've got our first down payment, cash received, hain't we?"

"But that's a long way from enough," said Arapaho. "Would you ride blindfolded through Comanche country, just because you'd been paid a few dollars in advance? We've got to know more about who is friend, and who is enemy. We'd better talk to this McIntosh, the foreman who hired us, like Mr. Southworth suggested."

They stabled their mounts at the livery and started down Main Street. A certain kind of dusk can come in the Northern Great Plains which Fane had heard, and believed, came nowhere else. The high arch of the sky, now entirely cloudless and sunless, was a crystal greenish blue, and the light in the streets and on the shopfronts, was definite, shadowless, as sort of smoky lavender.

This was supper time, and the boardwalk was deserted. Arapaho directed their first stop to The Stockman's Rest. There was a different barman on duty now, a greasy man who aped Freneau in pomade and dress, and who made no attempt to conceal his personal dislike for McIntosh. McIntosh had been there, spent the afternoon, and gone; he had come sober and left drunk. "He don't have to pay no bill, here." the barman said. "You might try the Eclipse. The same thing's true there. Though, to tell you the truth, I can't see why you, nor nobody else, could ever want even to look at him."

"What do you mean?" said Fane. "He doesn't have to pay any bill?"

"Some kind of an agreement he's got with his boss, Mr. Southworth. The place gets it, all right, but Mr. Southworth takes up the slack."

"How dare he even come in here?" asked Crezavent. "With all this bad friendship between those two partners?"

"They ain't no bad friendship between them two," said the barman quickly. "All that's jest ugly rumor."

Out again on the boardwalk, Arapaho said dryly, "And a free drink is always worth a little risk, isn't it? So let's try the Eclipse, like he said."

McIntosh had come and gone at the Eclipse, too. And was about as well liked in this place as he had been at The Stockman's Rest. Here, they chatted a little with a few bystanders. McIntosh, they heard, was loyal to his boss and the Box S, was a wizard and very good with cows, good with a drink of whiskey if he was paying for it, very good with it if there was no expense involved. "You'll find him at Miss Maribelle's," they were advised assuredly.

Miss Maribelle's, they discovered, was the structure referred to as the 'domicile' on Front, between Oak and East.

68

They found it, facing the railroad tracks. It wasn't a domicile and had certainly never been a domicile; it had probably been built as a short two-storied warehouse. It was of brick with a band of four windows in two rows, first and second stories; night had fallen by now and each window was lit from the light of kerosene lamps behind pale yellow blinds. The windowpanes were sooty from the belching of passing locomotives. There were cards in some of the upstairs windows, carefully lighted, though, each card saying the same thing, the common password known to every male: *Millinery*. If the cards portrayed the actual trades of the inmates, there were enough milliners in this one small building to outfit the heads of every hat fancier in three counties. It was a good location, for it stared the railroad station in the face and was immediately available to any gentlemen temporarily disembarking from the cars. The bulk of its customers, however, trailhands, gamblers, locals who simply felt the wish to listen to a piano, needed no window cards.

And piano music was coming out now, loud and gay and tinny, through the sooty warped door lintel, through even bricks and mortar, it seemed, like empty tin cans being kicked around by merry drunken squaws.

"It looks nice and solid," said Crezavent admiringly. "Like a nice place to go, say, if a cyclone or blizzard hit the town."

"I can think of better," said Arapaho. "Watch yourself every minute, and I'm not referring to *parfoom de Paree*."

Arapaho slipped his gun a couple of times in its holster, to give it the gunfighter's loosen; Crezavent automatically followed suit, Fane simply looked stolid, and they stepped inside.

They found themselves in a small, square hall. Facing them, ascending, were stairs, dirty, padded. To their left, through double doors, they could see the parlor, the place that gave such an establishment its name, a girl on a cheap couch along the opposite wall, unaccompanied except for a cat on her lap, the social center focus of the 'social center'. From this room, off to one side, out of sight, the piano was having its convulsions.

They had hardly passed the threshold when someone behind Fane tread on his boot heels, pushing inside past him.

It was Sheriff Sandy Sanderson, scrawny and grim as usual, with deputies. When he recognized Arapaho and Crezavent and Fane, he said in passing, "I'm gettin' to like you boys less and less. What you doing here? I know about you now."

"We came here to wait for a train," said Crezavent.

"I only wish I could believe it," said the sheriff.

"Mr. Southworth wants us to have a word with his foreman, McIntosh," said Arapaho. "Cattle."

"McIntosh, yes. Cattle, no," said Sanderson. "With me standing around, and for other reasons, I doubt if he'll talk to you, but come along."

The group ascended the stairs and came into a hall. The first door was open, and they entered and became part of a bleak scene. There was no bed in this room,

70

probably the only room on the floor that had no bed, Fane reflected, but bare walls and stark simple chairs around a simple table; on the table, as on the table Fane had glimpsed at the Eclipse, cards, loose coins, and banknotes. Around the walls were standing a few people, grave, some a little frightened, all silent: Maribelle herself, hatchet-faced, grotesque with her customary facial smudging of rice powder and thick rouge; four mighty hard case characters in work range clothes; and Fred Freneau, hair glistening, his black bone-handled cross-draw gun held muzzle down, arm full length. There was the smell of cigar in the air, and the faint smell of powder too.

On the floor, on elbows and knees, rump in the air, in a pool of blood, frozen in death, was McIntosh, chunky face half concealed, batwing chaps rumpled, his gun out of its holster, half showing from beneath his knee.

"What happened, I mean exactly?" asked the sheriff. "One of your girls, Miss Maribelle, came running to the courthouse with a kind of mixed-up picture, but I mean exactly?"

"I shot him," said Freneau. "Fair play. As each of these five people will testify."

He proffered his weapon, butt first, but the sheriff refused it. "Keep it, Fred," he said. "Nobody needs your gun, not at this point certainly. Anybody want to tell the story?"

"He was sitting here, playing cards, drinking," said Freneau. "Loading up on free drinks. Then he got the idea of a girl and sent for Miss Maribelle," said

Freneau. "She talked to him and then sent for me. We had a few words and then I shot him, fair play."

"What were those words?" asked the sheriff curiously.

"First, we talked about the girl. He wanted her free. I couldn't have did that even if I wanted to, which I surely didn't. The girls are friends of Miss Maribelle, and under her motherly attention, personally."

When no response was made by anybody, Freneau said, "Free drinks, yes, though it's wormwood and gall to me. Free girls, no."

"Did he ever demand a free girl before?" asked the sheriff.

"No, Sandy, he didn't," said Freneau. "He's asked for small loans at my card table here, and I've give 'em to him, as long as he kept 'em small. But never before for no human being girl."

"All right," said the sheriff. "Then what?"

"One word led to another, and he stood up, threatening, and I invited him to draw. I admit I provoked him. I loathed and despised him and took no pains to hide it."

Provoking, everywhere, Fane knew, was allowed. If a man didn't like it, he could always turn and walk away.

"So I let him touch his gun butt and then I shot him," said Freneau. "These people all saw it." He began a little lecture. "You can't beat a crossdraw. You shoot with your right hand, you see. In a crossdraw you move your right hand, muscles natural and —"

Now Fane noticed the four bystanders. Some of them were mildly amused by the lecture-character of the speech, some just wooden-faced.

Sheriff Sanderson said, "I know Miss Maribelle, of course, but who are these other men. I don't recollect ever seeing them before."

Now all the visitors looked at them. They were tough enough to make any ordinary tough, say one of the patrons of the Eclipse, look like a gentleman. It wasn't their clothes, their clothes weren't much, even for a drifter, and these men sort of had the feel of drifters about them, but there was just a chill of the inhuman and merciless about them. The first was wolf-jawed, teeth to match, long nose and slot-eyes. The second was very young, and the very young can be crazy-dangerous, Fane knew. The third and fourth looked like squat furry-throated apes, identical twins, certainly. The wolf-jawed man with the yellow teeth was apparently their leader, for they were obviously a unit.

He said, "It was jest like Mr. Freneau remarked. The other man was already half-drawed."

"And *my* remark," said Sheriff Sanderson, "was that I don't recollect any of you."

"We're jest four scrub cattlemen from Idyho," said the leader, "who was goin' a little traveling and heered the cheapest way to do it was by train and happened, by sheerest fate, to arrive in Polton in the same empty boxcar." He took out a roll of banknotes, flashed it, and shoved it back in his pocket. "We ain't troublemakin' vagrants or paupers, as you'll observe."

"Well," said Sheriff Sanderson amiably. "Welcome to Polton, and be good boys. And remember there's always empty boxcars running out of Polton as well as in."

"Need me any more?" asked Miss Maribelle.

The sheriff said no, and she left the room.

Then, to the four strangers he said, "If you boys would like to start your non-troublemaking good works right from start, the four of you could carry the body downstairs. Mr. Freneau will inform the undertaker. He will doubtless also inform Mr. Southworth."

"The least I can do," said Freneau. "My duty, you might say."

The four men carried the body from the room. The sheriff and his deputies started to follow. Crezavent said, "Funny thing I didn't hear no names mentioned."

"Why put 'em to the inconvenience o' lying?" said the sheriff, and left with his officers.

Now, to Arapaho, Fane, and Crezavent, Freneau said, "Would you gents step this way a minute, please."

CHAPTER
EIGHT

At the end of the hall was a door, and they entered, tailing Freneau cautiously inside, alert. They were in an office with a rolltop desk at their left. Freneau lighted a coal-oil lamp, fiddled with its wick until the flame satisfied him, killing time, trying to put them on edge, they knew, and then swung around the desk chair and seated himself, facing them.

He said, "I know you represent the opposition, the man who has set himself up as opposition, but I'm going to take you into my confidence."

"Whatever you want," said Arapaho. "But first I'd like you to look at Mr. Crezavent here."

Jolted a little, Freneau gazed at Crezavent.

Arapaho said, "You have just inspected, in my opinion, the greatest fancier of the female gender that lives, was ever born, or ever will be born."

"Correct," said Crezavent, flattered.

"And with Mr. Crezavent," said Arapaho, "I'd say card playing took second place in line."

"Correct again," said Crezavent.

"Yet I state it," said Arapaho, "as a simple fact that Mr. Crezavent, or any other man in a game of draw poker — if it was such — that neither Mr. Crezavent nor any other man would have the thought of womankind bear down on him at such a moment."

"Like poker, they have their time and place," said Crezavent, agreeing, but cautiously, showing puzzlement about what this was all about.

"Therefore," said Arapaho, "before we go into anything else, I think I should tell you I don't believe a damned word in your story about why you gunned down Mr. McIntosh."

"That's what I was coming to," said Freneau. "That's why I called you in here, that's what I wanted to talk to you about. And when you hear my story in confidence, if you've got any manhood in you, the three of you, you'll simply go to your livery stable, and get your horses and ride out of town and not mess in this."

"Did you tell this story to the sheriff?" asked Arapaho. "I don't seem to remember your doin' such."

"I'll tell it in court if I have to," said Freneau. "If it ever comes to that, but it won't."

All the while, ever since they had first seen him in the other room, Fane now realized, he had held his left hand cupped, as though he carried something, loosely.

And he had carried something, for now he opened his hand and laid an object on his knee. It was a little band of thin gold, about the diameter of a broomstick.

"What's that?" asked Arapaho.

"That's evidence, if it ever *does* come to court," answered Freneau.

"Now I understand," said Arapaho. "And you want us as witnesses that we saw it right afterwards, and you explained it to us."

76

Crezavent, surprising everyone with a bit of information about such an item, said, "That there's a baby bracelet."

It lay there, so innocent looking, on the sporty crosshatch of the man's knee cloth.

"I have to go back a couple of years," said Freneau. "Two years ago my brother, Ernie, and me were a pair of barbers with our own little two-chair shop way down in Yuma. We sold out and come north here to Polton, and started the Eclipse. It was Ernie's idea.

"He was a man of granite, with ambition. He picked up Miss Maribelle, stranded at the railroad station, and with what she told him, he began to expand. Next he set her up here, in her millinery business. Next, the high-fashion bug bit him and he started The Stockman's Rest. These projects, while showing good signs of prospering, overreached us after a while, with all the expansions, financially and faced us with bankruptcy and ruin. Miss Maribelle told us we simply had to have a little outside capital to tide us over, and we took in Southworth. Then, almost overnight, the money began pouring in."

"Maybe," said Arapaho, "it was Southworth's business judgement, too, that made things flourish."

"No, it was his capital," insisted Freneau. "Then, just when things were booming with us, Ernie was killed."

"Killed?" said Arapaho. "How?"

"Ambushed one stormy night coming back from a church barbecue in his buggy. He was shot in the back, and half robbed to fool me, but it didn't."

"Southworth did it, you think?" said Arapaho.

"Had it done. Southworth himself that night had a foolproof alibi. He was playing euchre with the sheriff."

"So you called it war, knowing the worst was to come, and brought in the Whistling Kid and Jarrett," said Arapaho.

Freneau shook his head. "I never seen nor heard of either of those gentlemen until they was laid out for the inspection of public delight. Bringing in gunthrowers is not a barber's trick — it's a rancher's."

"A minute ago you called us the opposition," said Arapaho. "What gave you that idea?"

"Southworth brought you in. You're a trio of these same type gunthrowers we was talking about."

"Why would he?" asked Arapaho.

"He would never admit as much, of course. But he went around town a time back saying here and there that they was an attempted bushwhack on him, too. Just after Ernie. But he outwitted it."

Now Fane got into the conversation.

"What's the bracelet?" he asked.

Freneau fondled it with a show of tender affection. He said, "It's Ernie's baby bracelet. He always wore it on his watch chain. It was among the things missing from his body. As soon as I saw it — McIntosh, drunk, had throwed it into a poker pot — I finally knowed who had killed Ernie — McIntosh himself, Southworth's private pig."

"So then you provoked McIntosh," said Fane. "Maybe with your draw already started, and killed him. And made up the other story for the sheriff."

"What would you have done?" asked Freneau.

"Called the law," said Fane. "Let's get out of here."

"Yep," said Crezavent. "Let's go."

78

They left the room, went down the hall, down the stairs and out into the night.

The piano music still rattled and clanged behind them. A burst of cheap perfume engulfed them. The girl whom they had seen earlier, on the couch with the cat in her lap, was standing on the doorstep, the cat now in her arms, ribbons and all.

In a low voice she said, "If you'll give me ten dollars, I've got two things I'll tell you boys."

"Fine," said Arapaho without hesitation.

"All right, give it," she said.

"In advance?" said Crezavent, sardonically.

But Arapaho was already handing it over. "I've bet on longer shots than this," he said. "What is it?"

"First," she said, "the way that man plays that piano turns my stomach."

"I agree so much," said Arapaho, "that you've already earned nine of those dollars. What's the other thing?"

"If Fred Freneau showed you a baby bracelet, it's mine not his. I'd showed it to him one time, and he came and got it from me about a half hour ago. About a minute after he saw Mr. McIntosh go upstairs to the card room. Is that worth the ten dollars?"

When they said nothing, she said, "I'll deny all this, of course. But I just thought that I'd let you boys leave here happy."

Arapaho led them not back to Main, but down Front.

"I could stand Mother's Eatery about now," said Fane.

"Mother's Eatery must wait a little," said Arapaho.

79

"You know who really killed McIntosh," said Crezavent. "I didn't see it, and he's well covered for it, but it was Jacky. It has to be Jacky. They say he's just like me, if they's any killing to be done, he's the one who does it. Even if Freneau and McIntosh half drawed together, Jacky, workin' now for Freneau, outdrawed them both and done it."

"Why do you say that, all that?" asked Fane.

"You mean about Jacky DeSana? Because it's only right to give credit where credit's due."

"He means about the working for Freneau part," said Arapaho.

"They was pointed out to me, when I got up to Split Butte before you other fellas," said Crezavent. "I was in a barnloft, and they come ridin' by, and they was pointed out to me, and named. It was them that was brought up from Colorado to damage Mr. Baldecker. They was Teddy Clark, the Flenner twins, and Jacky DeSana, the boy, the one we just was talking about. The only one I'd met was Jacky, whom I met in a card game under a railroad bridge outside of Trinidad."

"I've heard of 'em all," said Arapaho. "My, my."

"I missed them up at Split Butte," said Fane. "But I've got them now."

"Unavoidably," said Crezavent with a wicked grin. "Life is funny, hain't it?"

CHAPTER
NINE

As they strode through the light of the early moon, Fane said, "Do you think they recognized us?"

"Had to," said Crezavent. "They've stayed alive this long hain't they? That would be a major part of their trade, keeping posted."

"Then why wasn't there a fracas with them?" asked Fane.

"Wrong place," said Arapaho patiently. "Furthermore, that isn't the way a professional likes it."

"Who was the one with a face like a mean dog?" asked Fane.

"That was Teddy Clark," said Crezavent. "The way I heard it up north, he was the boss of the bunch."

"Offhand," said Arapaho thoughtfully, "offhand, I'd say he must be the worst of the lot."

"I'd say so, too," said Crezavent. "And then I'd place them stumpy lookalikes, the Flenner twins, next. They cain't read, they cain't write, they cain't even count their fingers."

They listened, attentively.

"But you send them out on a job," said Crezavent. "And they go out and do that job. And got the bullet scars to prove it."

Neither of his audience answered.

He said, "One is called Blue Ash and the other Buddy. They're mighty hard to tell apart, and when you come right down to it, why bother?"

"Well," said Arapaho. "I won't say yes or no for sure, but we may be looking at them again in about three minutes, and this time over gun muzzles."

When they turned into the alley from Front toward Main, and midway up its length came to the blacksmith shop, it loomed big, cumbersome, a hulk of blackish gray in the powdery moonlight. At the rear, a shanty-like structure was appended, showing only a smudge of light, a window beside a door. This was Mr. Jones' habitation, obviously as he was the proprietor. There were no horses in view in the moonlight, neither the bay described by Crezavent, nor any others.

"I can't say I like its looks," said Fane.

"You," said Arapaho, jerking his thumb at Crezavent, "go over and sit on yonder side of that wagon in that patch of shadow. If callers come, you stop them; the way you do it depends on the caller. Fane, you come in with me. It looks peaceful, but you never can tell what you'll find behind a door, any door."

Silently, Crezavent left them.

Arapaho knocked at the door, and they entered in one sweep, as though they had been invited in, which they hadn't.

The single dirt-floored room, stinking with horses and the fetid odor of a nearby outside privy, was walled with makeshift scraps and patches of secondhand planking.

The light was dim. Jones, the smith, exactly as Crezavent had described him, bow-legged, tough as whit leather, a little grizzled, too, and wet-lipped, stood at a cast-iron barrel-shaped stove ladling his supper, beans and lumps of sow belly, from a soot-stained canister-cauldron into a bowl made of the bottom of a small galvanized bucket roughly sheared down to size. Putting it on a barrelhead and seating himself on a stool up to it, he said, "Sorry gents that I can't ask you to join me, but this is sole and only for the man that works here."

"We didn't come to eat," said Arapaho good-humoredly.

"What did you come for?" asked the smith, showing only a tinge of interest in them.

"To take a look at you, for one thing," said Arapaho.

"Why is that?" asked the smith.

"Because I have a feeling you know us but we don't know you."

"That could be," said the smith. "The way you've been flouncing around, showin' off since you hit town, everbody knows you."

Reproachfully, Arapaho said. "Now that's a sorry way to put it. When if things had gone another way we'd be maybe good friends, working for Fred Freneau, like, if we want to go a little in the past, the Whistling Kid and Jarrett."

Unfazed, the smith gulped down a chunk of pork fat. He said, "Brother, you talk too quick for me."

"You've been doing Fred Freneau's heavy-gun recruiting for him in this little fuss, and that means you must have an interesting past yourself, by the way," said

Arapaho. "You know who they are, and where to go at the moment to get it."

"How could I find out such as that?" said the smith quizzically.

"I won't say you received personal letters from them to that effect," said Arapaho. "But the more I think about it, the more I wonder if the same couldn't be true. But there's another way, maybe even a smarter way, which I've known to be done on occasions, an even more reliable way, which you might very well use — but I don't think I'll mention it."

There was no expression whatever on the smith's face.

"You went up to Split Butte," said Arapaho, "and talked to Crezavent, but Crezavent said he'd already had a heap better offer from McIntosh."

"From Southworth, you mean?"

"Let's say McIntosh. But you managed to snag the others — Teddy Clark and his boys, the Flenners and Jacky DeSana."

"I deny it," said Jones, the smith. "I never even heard of any of them before, except Teddy Clark. He's well knowed of, o' course."

Dimly, from outside, came the sound of walking horses, two of them. They walked up to a short distance beyond the door, stopped, and then walked on.

Inside, all of them stood listening. When they had gone the smith said, "They would have jest wasted their time if they'd got down. I never shoe no horses at night, never. That's one good thing about being your own boss. You kin set yourself your own work hours."

84

Arapaho said, "I guess that's all. Let's amble on, Mr. Fane."

Out in the moonlight, Crezavent's form arose from behind the wagon and he came forward at a leisurely pace and joined them. As they left and turned once again into the alley, he said, "There were two of them. You said stop them according to the callers, and they didn't dismount, and weren't callers, so I didn't stop them. Did I do right?"

"Yes," said Arapaho.

"I always do right," said Crezavent.

"Tell me about them," said Arapaho.

Crezavent said, "They rode up to the window, looked in and rode on. That's all."

"What did they look like?" asked Arapaho. "Teddy Clark, or some of his bunch, maybe?"

"No," said Crezavent. "One was flat-faced, dressed in old mixed-up army clothes; that was DeLuxe Harrigan. The other was Tennessee O'Brien."

"South Texas gunthrowers," Arapaho explained to Fane. "I heard they were in Old Mexico, each of them."

"How can he be so sure?" asked Fane. "They just came and went. Only moonlight and lamplight and such a short time, too."

"If he says so, it's good enough for me," said Arapaho.

Crezavent said, "I shared a leg iron with Tennessee in Arizona once, and me and DeLuxe, county labor, helped put in a culvert in Wyoming. Accordin' to them, they're pretty wonnerful; accordin' to me, I've seen better."

"What does it mean?" asked Fane.

"It means Fred Freneau is in this thing to win, it looks like," said Arapaho. "It means he's still recruiting."

When no one answered, Arapaho said, "It's only a guess on my part, but I'd say we had four against us and now we're going to have six. Six to three."

"But we've always got Fane," said Crezavent. There was enough acid in his voice to dissolve a nail.

They left the far end of the alley at Main, and turned on Main toward Mother's Eatery. This was the town's social hour, and people, about the town's entire population, male and female of all ages, were in motion in the business section or standing before storefronts and at the edge of the boardwalk, visiting. The light touch of the breeze was pleasantly cool. They'd gone scarcely a hundred feet when Fane felt a touch at his sleeve and turned.

It was Miss Linda Southworth, whom they had seen that brief instant when they had been out at Southworth's ranch. He didn't recognize her at first, but — golden hair, golden eyes, golden skin — he remembered her on the instant after. Crezavent, nervous as always when sudden unexplainable tension replaced his typical serenity, was about a block ahead. As Fane slowed up at the touch, Arapaho politely continued on.

He said, "Good evenin', Miss Southworth."

She said, "Mr. Fane, I must speak to you privately. It's very urgent." She did, in fact, look breathless.

He said, "Is it about me, personal, or about this mix-up someway?"

"It's about this mix-up, as you call it."

"Then Arapaho will have to listen in," said Fane. "We're all in this together." He called: "Arapaho!"

Arapaho stopped, turned and walked back. He stood quietly, courteously.

She said, "If you get in a jam, say Miss Amanda *and the three children*."

With a quirk to his lip, Fane said, "What is this? The Mystic Order of the Knights of Something-or-other?"

Arapaho said with gravity, "Don't tease the young lady, Fane. Can't you see she's trying to do you a good deed?"

"*Miss Amanda and the three children*," said Fane. "How will that help?"

"I'm not trying to help you," she said, but without conviction. "Not really. The truth is, I'm acting against my better judgement. I should have nothing whatever to do with any of you. Your presence is just a curse to Papa."

And then she was swiftly gone.

They looked at each other, shrugged, and continued down the crowded street.

They caught up with Crezavent standing at the outside fringes of a little crescent of people — townsmen, cowboys, loafers — in front of the Eclipse saloon. "At least," said Arapaho as they came up, "at least he's outside, not inside." They paused at Crezavent's side. A game of Mumble-de-peg was being played. This game was played on wood. If you wanted to gamble on something, here was a game of skill, and skill only, with no possible way of being rigged. On a long wooden bench, used in daytime by folks with time on their hands who liked to sit and watch the parade of the world pass by, sat two men, one at each end, facing each other. They were a couple of sun-scorched, slightly tipsy cowhands, each with his month's wages on the bench in front of him, their game lighted by an extra lamp placed in the saloon window for their benefit, compliments of the establishment.

The knife was that most common ordinary of all jackknives, a Barlow, with both blades at one end. It had been opened this way, the big blade full out, straight with the handle, the small blade half out, perpendicular to the big blade and handle, making a sort of T, with the small blade the T's stem. The small blade was then stuck in the wood lightly, and the knife flipped forward, spinning, into the air. The game was played in the line of the grain of the wood.

The knife went up into a small arc, spinning, and lit. If it failed sticking when it lit, the count was nothing. If it stuck with knife butt and small blade touching the wood, the count was twenty-five. If it stuck with small blade and large blade touching the wood, the count was seventy-five. On small blade alone, count fifty. On large blade alone, count one hundred. It was a game much played and practiced in livery stables and line camps to while away the tedium.

These men were both experts, never missing the one hundred position, and if it were not for the dazzle of the money in view, the watchers wouldn't have punished themselves with the monotony. And of course there were always local records to tie or beat, and that, Fane knew, was a point of interest to many in the audience.

A man pushed his way into them, head down, using his shoulders a little too freely, maybe. It was Southworth, and Fane, seeing this different aspect of him, this doggedness, knew how he had amassed enough capital ranching to buy into town investments. Another feeling came over Fane, too: Freneau was up against a really formidable man.

"Just step into this doorway a minute," Southworth said. They followed him into the recessed entry of a shop, closed for the night. He said, "I've been looking for you ever since I got the word about my foreman. I want to see you."

"I want to see you, too," said Arapaho. "I'm uneasy about this whole thing. We've taken your money but we've had no orders from you — you or anyone else. What are we supposed to do? Just walk around and get shot? This kind of dodge isn't our trade. We're range men."

"You've got orders now," said Southworth bleakly. "I want Fred Freneau dead by morning."

"Yes, sir," said Crezavent.

"No, sir," said Arapaho. "I don't do things that way."

"I do," said Crezavent. "I've took your money, Mr. Southworth, and I'll give value received, just as you lay it out. Arapaho, you and Mr. Slow-Draw-but-Dead-Shot-Fane here, go to your hotel room, take off your boots, and relax. You'll be seeing me a little later."

"And when you go to that hotel room," said Southworth, "be sure to bolt that door."

"I always do," said Fane. "I got in the habit because my mother always bolted doors. But what are you getting at?"

"I just left a message for Fred Freneau with the barman at The Stockman's Rest," said Southworth. "And the way I put it, he knew mighty well I meant what I said. I said Fred Freneau is going to be sorry he shot down my Box S foreman. I said tell Fred Freneau he's going to be dead himself by morning."

Warningly, Arapaho said, "You'd better simmer down, Mr. Southworth. You wouldn't stand a chance with the crowd he's got around him."

Southworth ignored him. He said, "You should have seen the barman's hand shake. I told him I was just carrying a message — that it came from you gentlemen."

Fane flushed angrily. Crezavent smiled. Arapaho said, "Well, that fixed it, all right. I wouldn't want to swear one way or the other, but Fred Freneau or not, somebody will be deceased by morning. That's sure."

And now Southworth, like his daughter a few minutes earlier, was gone, swallowed by night and people.

Somehow, Fane realized to his amazement, he wasn't in the least frightened. Just prickling with awareness, just under a lightning tension, like great unexpected emergencies had put him many times before.

A voice said, "All right, boys, jest take it easy."

Sheriff Sandy Sanderson and his two deputies joined them. The same two slightly undersized, slightly prune-faced deputies. The sheriff and his men were deadly serious, their guns out but relaxed. Fane and his companions froze.

Deputy hands came out and removed their gun belts.

"Come along," said the sheriff.

"To where?" asked Fane.

"Courthouse," said the sheriff curtly.

"Without our six-guns," said Arapaho, "we'll never make that walk alive. We've just got word that a match has been tossed in the powder keg, and we pass a lot of windows and doors and people."

"The man that shoots a prisoner in my custody," said Sheriff Sanderson very gently, "will come to regret it."

"Somehow that doesn't cheer me the way it should," said Fane politely.

"Did I hear you say prisoner?" asked Arapaho.

CHAPTER
TEN

There was a small room upstairs in the courthouse. It wasn't exactly a questioning room, but Fane sensed in his bones a lot of questioning had taken place there. It was a room which no one had so far got around to finishing. There were a few broken toys piled in a corner, but it wasn't a playroom. Its floor was bare but in the center was a round-topped mahogany table with jagged strips of veneer gone from the top; around the table were three chairs, stout hickory kitchen chairs. Fane and his companions were seated. The two deputies stood sleepily alert by the inside of the door jamb, the sheriff was here and there, restively.

At a signal from the sheriff, one of the deputies left the room and returned with a blowzy looking individual carrying a stage whip, who inspected them as though they were crawling with insects, nodded, and got out in a rush.

"You saw him affirm," said the sheriff. "Now we can get down to business."

Whatever this was, Fane knew, it was bad.

"That was Ben Parsons," said the sheriff. "When was the last time you saw him?"

"I don't recall ever seeing him before, at all," said Fane. Arapaho and Crezavent, wiser in the words of sheriffs, said nothing.

"He's driver for the Swinnerton Line which runs south out of here, our only line," said the sheriff. "Any of you gents ever see a Swinnerton coach?"

"I saw one in front of the hotel about an hour ago," said Fane.

"Don't get funny with me," said the sheriff kindly. "It won't make things any easier for you."

He made himself a cigarette out of a piece of brown wrapping paper and tobacco, hinterland style, an instrument that would kill an ordinary human, and got it going.

"Earlier tonight," said the sheriff, "Ben Parsons was drivin' his stage north, on its last lap, toward Polton. It was just about dusk-dark, a little more on the night side than daylight. He had one passenger, a windmill drummer. The passenger was on the back seat. Was on the back seat then, now he's laid out with Mr. McIntosh, in the undertaker's workroom."

"I do believe," said Arapaho, entranced, "that he's got it in his mind to hang us for killing a windmill drummer. Or am I getting ahead of the story?"

"You keep out of this and shut up," said the sheriff in a tone like sandpaper. "You don't fit into this in no way whatever, and we don't want no free-gratis contributions from you."

A little auburn-haired girl about five years old came into the room, sorted through the pile of toys, picked up a rag doll, tucked it under her arm and left.

When she had gone, the sheriff continued: "The coach had just left Knucklebone Spring and was enterin' that crooked canyon just beyond, when this man" — he pointed at Fane — "and this man" — he pointed at Crezavent — "come ridin' up, and robbed coach, driver, and passenger."

At dusk-dark, they were all on the plain, returning from their visit at Southworth's ranch. And who could testify to that?

"And this Ben Parsons identifies them?" said Arapaho.

"Speak when you're spoke to," said the sheriff. "I don't want to have to tell you again."

"At dusk-dark we were on the prairie," said Fane.

"Not in bed?" said the sheriff. "Generally when you ask them, they've been in bed."

Back from the cells, dimly, someone was singing a hymn. For an instant there was no other sound.

The sheriff said, "The passenger, when it was all over, was still scared and got out and ran. This man" — he pointed again at Crezavent — "shot him. Gave him a little distance, and shot him. Shot him first in the leg to bring him down, and then put two into his head. For no reason whatever except marksmanship. This other man" — his thumb jerked toward Fane — "cut the horses from the harness and drove them off." Showing the edges of his teeth, he said, "And that's it."

"If it was dark," said Fane, "and it must have been dark, the way you've been trying to get around it, how can this man Parsons say for sure?"

"Maybe he's got cat eyes," said the sheriff.

94

"Or maybe you got some peculiar stink," said one of the deputies.

"It seems to me," said Crezavent, "when you come right down to it, you better give us back our guns and apologize. You got nothing whatever agin us."

"I got a murdered man and a witness to it," said the sheriff. "What more could anyone want?"

"That was the quickest identification I ever heard of," said Fane. "In and out like a rabbit."

"When he come in and reported it to me," said the sheriff, "I took him uptown, and you were among others I showed him."

"Is that going to be good enough for a jury?" asked Fane.

"It's good enough for my deputies," said the sheriff. "And they don't like unarmed men shot for marksmanship purposes. I only hope you reach a jury."

Crezavent looked like a caged bobcat. Fane's mouth felt dry as an empty canteen, and there's nothing drier.

Later he could never understand how it came to him, but he said, "Miss Amanda *and* the three children."

It was like taking a wonderful cold bath after a day digging post holes in August, to see the wince shatter the sheriff's calm. He said, "Would you please repeat that?"

And Fane did, neither adding to nor subtracting from it.

"You've been talking to Linda Southworth," said the sheriff.

"Yes," said Fane. "But how did you know?"

"Because my wife and Linda are like mother and daughter. And she would have told Linda. And Linda would have called her Miss Amanda, but you would have called her Mrs. Sanderson."

"What is this?" asked Crezavent. "What have you been holding back, Fane?"

"Boys," said the sheriff to his deputies. "This is going to come as news to you, too. But I tried."

"That's okay with us, boss," said one of the deputies, and there was the deepest of friendship in his voice. "Whatever you're talking about, it's okay with us."

The sheriff said, "When Parsons reported it, I took him uptown and pointed these men out, and brought him back here. We sat in the kitchen and talked about it a short spell, and he said no he didn't think so, and besides how could he be sure when it happened so quick and he was so scared and drunk and it was so dark. Amanda was cooking supper and the little ones was playing around. Finally, I talked him into saying yes, or anyway yes maybe."

Arapaho let out the longest breath Fane ever heard.

The sheriff put out his mammoth cigarette and carefully saved the tobacco. "Amanda got into the conversation. She said if I tried to arrest you for it, she'd go into court, she *and* the children, and say just what was what."

"But Parsons agreed, in spite of her, to come around to your point of view," said Fane. "To come in here and identify us."

"He agreed to come in and nod," said the sheriff. "How can you or anybody else say for sure what he was nodding at?"

"If you didn't really intend to try us," said Fane, "what was the idea?"

"The idea was to get you all out of town, and I mean right now!" said the sheriff. "I was going to waver after a bit, and tell you you could go to your hotel for an hour or so, until I picked up a little more evidence I had in mind. That would put you long gone, quick and far."

"You play rough," said Arapaho.

"This is a rough town," said the sheriff. "I keep law and order. I know now who you are, and what you're here for."

"Yet it was you who brought us to town," said Fane.

"I was tricked," said the sheriff, and they believed him. "When I brought in your pal, Crezavent here, I was tricked."

"May I ask," said Fane, "if you're with Freneau in this, against Mr. Southworth?"

"I'm not *against* anybody," said the sheriff. "I'm just trying to handle the status quo, and the status quo, just left alone, is bad enough. Fred Freneau is part of Polton's status quo, and Mr. Southworth, and the grief that's followed him in, is what you might call something different. You, for instance, aren't either."

When there was no reply, the sheriff said, "You'll be given back your guns and you kin go."

A little later, as they descended the stairs to the first floor, buckling their belts, Crezavent said, "It's my guess they was DeLuxe and Tennessee, just happening up, picking up a little easy money on their way into town, who shot the drummer. Could be anyone's choice with them two. Many's the time, though, that Tennessee's boasted to me how he always cut the harness and drove off the horses, but he told me a lot of other things I didn't too much believe."

"Maybe we'd better go back and inform the sheriff," said Fane.

"Maybe we'd better stay out of it," said Crezavent. "I, for one, have had enough of it."

Blue, Fane's gelding, had been a present from his wife. She had seen it, and liked the magnificent rangy animal, and had bought it for him, not for any special occasion, but just bought it, and of all the gifts he'd received, he treasured it the most. Back at Iraville, when he was away from home on Blue for any length of time, say down at the county seat, or anywhere else, he made it a practice to check up on the gelding once a day for sure, generally at early night, not only for a friendly chat, but to be certain everything was okay.

When they left the courthouse, on their way to Mother's Eatery, they stopped by at Fane's request.

A man's horse, Arapaho had explained to Fane, when a man is in our trade, can be as important to him as his gun. And when the moment for their need comes up, neither of them had better misfire. So when you were in town, you were mighty careful about the livery stable you selected. In a general way, you could say livery stables fell into two types: the type catering to what you might call the fancy trade, mainly renting out their own stock and vehicles, and what you might call boardinghouse type, putting more stress on care and feeding and grooming, and so forth, of guest horses that they were asked to put up. The services of both types were intermingled, of course, and it was up to you to use your judgement. What you wanted was the boardinghouse type, that was considerate and honest to your mount.

What you didn't want, had to stay away from like poison, was the places that went overboard with extra flashy rigs-to-hire, stylish horses-to-hire. There were some pretty cruel ways to make a horse show spirit and style under the reins, and an outfit that would do that to their own horses, a place like that, cared nothing and less than nothing for your horse.

They entered by the front from the sidewalk, passed the open door of an office foul with tobacco juice and crumpled papers, and came into a long plank-floored room lined on either side with compartmented stalls, some with their doors open, some with them closed. At intervals down its length, from high on rough hewn posts, hung lanterns. At the far rear, double doors with a shallow ramp to the outside, were spread to the blackness of the backyard and the night.

They had scarcely gone down the floor a third of its length when Crezavent said urgently under his breath, "The roan! In that open stall to our left. The Whistling Kid's bay. The one I saw in the blacksmith's shop, getting a new set of shoes. The one you explained to me about later, Arapaho!"

Arapaho retorted almost inaudibly, "Later. Leave it to me, later."

They went to the stall which held Fane's gelding, and waited while he talked to it a bit, and patted it.

They had just left the stall, and were standing in the center of the livery, when the stable owner, a hunched knobby-cheeked man who looked half horse himself, came up to them and said, "Any of you gentlemen interested in buying a good horse?"

Arapaho, who didn't want or need one, but was always interested in looking at and discussing a good horse anytime, said, "I won't say yes and I won't say no. Where is it?"

Half-turning, the stableman pointed to the roan. "Yonder."

The group of them, all of them, started in that direction.

Inside the stall, Crezavent, the last one in, closed the door behind them, big enough to see out, but scarcely big enough to notice anything inside. Crezavent like Arapaho, Fane had noticed, never took any chances.

With the stall door closed, the stall was dim. The stable owner said, "I want you to see right good what's comin' to you. We'd better have a little more illumination on the subject." He fussed with a lantern, dark, on a peg on the wall. He had taken off the chimney and was cleaning the charred wick with his thumbnail, when Fane went stiff.

Through the slot in the door, he saw two men pass on the far side of the stable floor. One was Jacky DeSana, the vacant-eyed, rosy-cheeked youngster, the one who Crezavent had said was just naturally kill-crazy, and the other, wicked-faced, vain in highly polished brass wherever he could put it on, belt conchos, belt buckle, spurs, even hatband buckle, strode arrogantly beside him. This second man was a stranger to Fane. They had come from the back and were headed for the front, peering as they walked, up to the loft, down, here, there, left and right. They passed from sight.

The stable owner got his lantern going and the mare stood out before them, a splendid animal they all realized.

"What's her name?" asked Fane. This seemed like a trivial question, but every real horseman knew a mount responded not only to a familiar voice, but to a name, every bit as much as a child.

"Name's Hungry," said the stable owner, grinning.

They all grinned in response.

"Ever see one that wasn't?" asked Crezavent.

"Hello, there, Hungry," said Fane.

"No offense," said Arapaho, "but you got a bill of sale?"

"Certainly," said the liveryman, disappearing, and reappearing with a paper.

A sale without a bill of sale, was mighty dangerous for the buyer. It was his safeguard, his legal proof that he had bought the horse, that he hadn't stolen it. But there was something else to a bill of sale; it passed on from owner to owner with the horse, and thus contained a list, a sequence of all previous owners.

It was this item, Fane and Crezavent knew, which interested Arapaho.

And now, at the very instant when the paper changed hands, from the liveryman to Arapaho, the liveryman exploded his bombshell. He tried to do it in a casual way. He said, "They's only one name on the paper. The previous paper got lost somehow."

Got lost somehow. How many times that had been said before. And almost always when the deal was questionable.

However, it seemed to faze Arapaho not at all. He said, even before he glanced at it, "It's not yours, o' course. You're just the agent?"

"Jest the agent," said the liveryman.

And then Arapaho looked at it: *For the sum of one dollar and other considerations* (the customary phrasing of any bill of sale, to keep the new buyer from knowing what the owner himself had paid for it) . . . all perfectly legal, all in order, with two names however at the bottom, not one: Fred Freneau, seller, Maribelle Browne, buyer and present owner.

They had to do it that way, of course, Arapaho intimated, showing it to Fane. There couldn't have been any bill of sale at all, if the present owner hadn't bought it.

"It must have been Mr. Freneau that lost the previous bill of sale," said Arapaho, returning the document.

"Oh, I shouldn't think so," said the liveryman, obviously a decent human. "That doesn't sound like Mr. Freneau, losing things."

"Then what happened?" asked Arapaho. "Did he go up along the Milk and catch it himself? You'll have to admit it don't scarcely look like no wild young mustang."

"Mr. Freneau will stand behind it, you all know that," said the stableman. "And he wouldn't have took it in the first place if he hadn't knowed it was legal and would stand up in court. A gentleman like Mr. Freneau runs into some funny situations."

"This Maribelle Browne," said Arapaho. "That wouldn't be Miss Maribelle, the shop owner, would it?"

"Yes, it would," said the stableman with a chip on his shoulder. "And if you've got any slurring remarks to make on the subject, be good enough to leave my premises before you make 'em."

"How much are you asking?" said Fane.

They all looked at him, Arapaho, with surprise.

"Well," said the stableman, suddenly becoming the most skilled of all artists to them — the horse trader. "It's a one price deal, no haggling. It's not cheap, because she ain't a cheap mare. But it ain't high, because Miss Maribelle jest mainly wants her moved. The price I was told to ask, and stick by, is one hundred twenty-five."

Crezavent shook his head pitifully. Fane said, "Would you step out and let us talk this over?" (You always shook your head.)

The stableman nodded, and stepped out.

When the door was closed, this time firmly, Fane said, "Let me tell you what I just saw." He told them of Jacky DeSana and his brass glittering companion.

Arapaho's face remained stolid. Angrily, Crezavent said, "See what you teamed us up with Arapaho? Yellow as they come."

Fane said, "They were looking for us. I didn't want them to find us. Not here, of all places. Gunfire and the smell of fresh blood would be a nightmare to half the horses in this stable for the rest of their lives. Most of the horses here are town horses. And besides, I didn't want any of these horses shot, any."

"And besides, you didn't want yorese'f shot," said Crezavent. He turned to Arapaho, "The man with Jacky was Tennessee. Like you said, they've joined forces."

"All right!" Arapaho called. "Come back in, Mister."

The liveryman rejoined them. "Well?"

"Mr. Fane here finds himself interested," said Arapaho. "But he'd like to think it over."

"That's reasonable enough," said the liveryman. "But I can't guarantee to hold the mare."

"He understands," said Arapaho. "Let's go, boys."

On their walk down the stable floor toward the front door, Arapaho and Crezavent seemed to have forgotten the two searching gunmen already.

Arapaho said, "How did the horse get from Lyman Jones, the smith, to Miss Maribelle? That's a question and an interestin' one."

"Maybe," said Fane, "when the Whistling Kid died, Freneau claimed it and gave it to her."

"Or Jones hisself, give it to her."

"That's hard to believe," said Arapaho. "Remember, Jones wouldn't even give a couple of visitors, me and Fane, any of his sorry beans and pork."

"She must have bought it, bargain price, from one of them," suggested Crezavent.

"Or her name on the paper was just a cover for Freneau," said Arapaho. "Well, anyway you look at it, it ties the Whistling Kid up with the Fred Freneau bunch, beyond all doubt. As if we needed it."

The moon was up outside, as they stepped from the doorstep onto the walk, up big and round and white with a power of brilliance so strong you could see the knots and even part of the grain in the weathered doorframe behind them. Up and down the street, things, buildings and tied wagons and such, seemed of frosted ice. Cubed and diagonalized with geometric shadows, velvet black some places, indigo and lettuce-green in others. On either side of the livery building was a wide alley; these were the most commonly used means of entry into the building, down the alleys, around, and in through the rear.

Arapaho, like a general, said, "Crezavent, you stay right here. Fane, you take that alley, I'll take this, and we'll meet at the back. Fane, watch yourself."

"Why?" asked Fane. "What are we up to?"

"Jacky and his friend," said Arapaho. "If they're looking for us, then we're looking for them. I want to be sure they've moved on before we move on."

Expostulating, starting to argue, Fane said, "Why trouble still waters?"

"Because, though it don't seem so, this way is safer, my friend," said Arapaho. "Because things have changed. Because it's over the edge. And because a job's a job."

Without another word, Fane wheeled and started down the alley.

Behind the building was an open space, perhaps half the size of a town block. About half of this, to the far rear, was a corral enclosed by a lodgepole fence. Faint yellow light stained the air from the open backdoors of the stable; in the brilliant moon it was hardly more than a golden dusty diffusion. Between the corral and the building were vehicles for hire, either with or without teams, buckboards, buggies, a hauling wagon or two. As Fane rounded the alley corner and came into it, the very lonesomeness of it all reminded him of tombstones, and the Iraville graveyard at night.

When they came up to him, they were just there, abruptly. He, in his boyhood, had been a trailer and a tracker, and a stalker, but of game. But game, surprised, ran; it didn't shoot, and maybe ran better than you could. These, on occasion, were stalkers of men, and always dangerous men. He was entirely unaware of them until one of them spoke.

They stood to his left, about ten feet behind him, Jacky DeSana and his cheap friend of glittering brass. Slowly, he turned and faced them squarely. They stood at ease, thumbs hooked carelessly under the leather of their belts at their hip joints, fingers relaxed over the heavy cartridges which studded the belts, more like a couple of sociable friends than mad wolves.

To his companion, DeSana said, "Tennessee, this is one. The one I told you about. The dead shot."

If they knew dead shot, they knew slow draw, Fane realized. They were toying with him.

Fane said, expressing the startled truth, "I thought you searched the stable and left."

"Left and come back," said Jacky DeSana affably. "Man in the feed store across the street said he saw you go in, but never saw none of you come out."

They seemed so harmless.

Jacky DeSana said, "Tennessee, please stay out of this. In my day I've kilt about ever'thing — lice, stink bugs, maggots, but I've never kilt a dead shot yet. Mr. Fane, draw at your pleasure, and no hard feelings." There was a beast under that boyish skin of his face now, a mindless beast with glazed eyes. To Tennessee a different voice, flat and lifeless, added, "I always tell them that — no hard feelings."

Almost involuntarily, Fane started his draw.

CHAPTER
ELEVEN

Crezavent burst into the diffusion of yellow light from behind Fane. He came in a rush of bunched muscle (to shorten his lethal range, he later explained), left arm stiffly out from the shoulder, as though he were trying to fly, his drawn gun leeched tight against his pelvis, blazing. It was like a sharpshooter shooting from a moving horse, and his shots, four of them, in coughing orange flashes from his gun muzzle, seemed nearly to come all at once, like three separate men loosing a volley together at a turkey shoot.

The first two shots, he explained later to Arapaho, got Jacky DeSana in the belly, to take away his enthusiasm, quick and for sure; the next, when he was a little better steadied, dead center in Tennessee's upper eyelid to kill him, and then a mercy shot for Jacky.

And now Arapaho was with them. "I was slowed up a little," he explained. "Taking a look-see into a shed."

DeSana's gun, despite all, was drawn past its cylinder. Crezavent drew it the rest of the way out, held it to the light of the stable door, and examined it.

Fane, with his avid interest in guns, looked at it too. It was a Colt Lightning Model, 4½ inch barrel, .38 blue steel.

Crezavent said, "Gun model, caliber, and barrel length favored by Billy the Kid. But Jacky DeSana sure as hell wasn't no Billy the Kid, for several reasons."

He replaced it as carefully as he had got it, half in the dead man's holster.

Fane said, "What were you doing back here?"

"I was about to ask the same question," said Arapaho. "I stationed you out front."

"I was follerin' your blood brother here," said Crezavent. "I had a feelin' he was fixin' to cut and run and I wanted to call goodbye to him."

When no one said anything, Crezavent said, "Mr. Fane, I saved yore life. Ain't you even going to thank me for it?"

It's true, thought Fane. *Me against those two professionals. He saved it, all right.*

His face flaming with anger, Fane said, "Thank you."

Crezavent cleared his throat, hacking up a blob of phlegm, and spat it in the dust.

"That for your thanks," he said offensively, "and for you personally. Like Arapaho said, we're on a job."

Forty-five minutes later, they were in Mother's Eatery, just finishing their supper, spareribs and green beans and potatoes, cooked together with a liberal dosing of cayenne, served to them in huge individual blue bowls and tin pie pans as side plates for the bones. Dessert was a wedge of dried peach pie as thick as a man's wrist.

The sheriff, keeping himself carefully under control, had been dispassionate and fair. The man in the feed store across the street from the livery had told him DeSana and his pal had questioned him in a pretty nasty way, searching for Arapaho and his friends, obviously on the hunt for serious trouble. That was enough for anybody in Polton. It was enough for the sheriff. What his private feelings on the matter were, he didn't say, but he didn't bother even to detain them.

Using their tin soup spoons, they had just demolished the last of the pie, when the Chinese owner came to their table and said in a low voice that a person, a lady, had come in the back door and wished a word with them in a back room — a private word.

After a moment's hesitation, at a nod from Arapaho, they arose and followed the Chinese to the rear.

The walls in this room were covered with straw matting and a girl sat alone at a small table in the center of the floor. She was young, quietly dressed. But there was a kitten on the table, delicately eating the girl's ham sandwich, and the kitten was a furry little ball of ribbons, pink and baby blue, in pompoms and bows.

Arapaho said courteously, "I don't recognize you, ma'am. But I sure recognize your livestock. You must be the young lady with the kitten who stopped us on the doorstep of Miss Maribelle's and sold us that information."

"That's right," she said, and smiled, and it was a pretty nice smile, even Fane had to admit that.

"And I bet you want to sell us some more information?" said Arapaho.

"Correct," she said. "But this time the price is going to be double."

"This time, at that price," said Arapaho, "I hate to tell you, but the shop's closed."

"That's up to you," she said, and reached for her cat.

"Wait a minute," said Fane. "I'll stand treat this time. I trust this young lady." He placed coins politely before her.

She put the money in a tiny beaded purse, and said, "I do believe I've got enough saved up to buy me a farmer husband, if the fancy should take me. He won't be a cattleman, I can tell you that. Wheat, I think. I was raised with wheat, and still dream about it."

Crezavent simmered at the delay, but Fane said, "Give her time. She's scared. Let her get set."

"You bet I'm scared," she said. "Well, here it is. Find out about the time Miss Maribelle looked a judge in the eye. Let's say the last time. It's the only time I know about, anyways."

"How long ago was that?" asked Arapaho.

"About a year ago, I'd guess."

"Why?" demanded Crezavent.

"It might save your lives," she said simply.

"For what reason?" asked Arapaho.

"That's what you'll have to find out," she said.

"But nothing come of it, hey?" said Arapaho.

"Oh, didn't it?" said the girl. "She got the works."

"Where did it happen?" asked Fane.

"Right here in Polton."

"Then to find out," said Arapaho, "all we have to do is go to the courthouse and look it up in the records."

"Where and how you find out," she said, "is up to you. But you had better do it, before it's too late."

"It's too late already," said Crezavent. "Or hadn't you heard?"

She made no answer, but picked up her kitten and left.

They left the mat-walled room, went down the passage, into the big front main eating room.

At this hour it was almost deserted, but at a far table, just inside the front door, sat Sheriff Sandy Sanderson and his prune-faced deputies.

"Why not settle this right here and now?" said Arapaho. "Here's the law in person."

They veered to one side and came up to the sheriff's table. They were not welcomed cordially.

The sheriff said, "Don't tell me you got reasonable, and got yore heads together, and have come over to bid me farewell? Forever."

"No," said Arapaho. "We've come over to consult you on what I suppose you could call a line of duty."

"Your line of duty, or mine?" asked the sheriff dryly.

"Yours," said Arapaho.

"Then yo're wasting yore time," said the sheriff. "I have nothing whatever to say to you. I wouldn't give you, any of you, the time o' day. And as to discussin' my line of duty, you, none of you, ain't even citizens here."

"Let's hear what he has to ask," said one of the deputies. "I'm curious."

"Have you, or yore deputies, or the town marshal, or any of the law hereabouts, ever arrested Miss Maribelle?"

112

You could almost smell the scorch of the hot rage that went through the group of seated men.

"No," said the sheriff. "That's the answer to your question. Now I'm going to add something for your general health and welfare. Watch that kind of talk around here. That nice lady is so admired and respected she could be elected mayor."

"What a wonnerful idee," said Crezavent lasciviously. "That's jest the kind of town I'd like to settle in. And I bet she'd even bring her own courthouse along with her."

They ignored him.

Arapaho stubbornly went on. "I had information to the contrary. Then if she was never arrested, she could never have been convicted?"

"No," said the sheriff.

"Not even convicted and sentence suspended," said Arapaho.

"Yo're not only being insulting," said the sheriff, "but yo're talking silly at the same time. No arrest, no conviction, no suspended sentence."

"Do you know what we could do?" said one deputy to the other. "The boss could arrest them here and now for, say, disturbin' the peace. We could relieve them of their iron, and then, who knows what? I bet we could have a fearsome battle with them resisting an officer and maybe even attempting escape."

"And they might very well try it, too," said Arapaho. "Let's get back to the hotel."

As they departed, Fane wondered what next. What were Arapaho's plans, for he certainly had them. One thing, sure as heck, they weren't headed for the hotel, you could bet on that. The best guess was that Arapaho and Crezavent would start a little combing of the town themselves, as DeSana and Tennessee had been doing. But what then? Play it by ear?

But Fane couldn't bring himself to believe this, either. It wasn't like Arapaho to play anything by ear.

Outside, on the boardwalk, Arapaho looked suddenly electrified. "A J.P." he said. "O' course. A J.P."

CHAPTER
TWELVE

But what Arapaho did on leaving Mother's Eatery surprised them both, Crezavent as well as Fane. He went down Main Street, intruding apologetically into little knots of gossiping townsfolk saying over and over again, "Excuse me for interrupting, gentlemen, but where can I find a notary? This gentleman" — pointing to Crezavent — "is going to lease me his spare barn on shares."

Within a block, they learned that Polton had three persons empowered to notarize: the circuit judge who came and went with the sessions, absent during this period; the sheriff's wife, because many official documents had to be notarized when the sheriff was out in the county; and Old Doc Blount, doctor of nothing, who held his grubby makeshift hit-or-miss rural magistrate's court out at Turtle Creek, conveniently just a stone's throw beyond the town's actual boundary.

"That's our man, Justice of Peace Blount," said Arapaho. "She said it could save our lives, and she could be right. We'd better see him right now, before anything else."

They had been told how to get there, and that it was just a short walk, so they walked.

Crezavent grumbled all the way, but to Fane it was a respite, and he was feeling a heap better when they arrived. Seeing two men killed, as Crezavent had killed them, plus such a narrow escape, was not a pleasant experience.

The village of Turtle Creek, when you came right down to it, so they had been told, and so they found, consisted of nothing but a shallow ford, a shaky pole footbridge, erected by Doc Blount for his own usage mainly, and a piled-up-looking structure on the other side of the water, a half sod, half timber thing that looked like a fusion of a giant mud turtle carapace and a tepee, with three tin stovepipes sticking up through its earth roof. Lamplight came from a window deeply set in by the front door and from the open door itself.

They crossed the bridge and entered the open door. It was an unusual place inside, and even Crezavent gaped. It was surprisingly roomy, divided into two space sections, really, a sort of shop-living-quarters just inside the threshold, and to their left a kind of storage place for raw furs. All of it had been well floored, with sections of wagon beds, disassembled and refitted, a couple of barn doors cut down and patchworked in, and other wooden objects.

There were a few rough shelves, with only the most nonluxurious basic staples, and a little shelf, awkwardly placed high on the wall with a square of gunny sacking covering it, which Fane knew was a backwoods whiskey shelf, out of reach and out of temptation, as sometimes found in hinterland horse change stations and post office shops. But this place was no post office; it was a threadbare trading station — it had to be, with those furs.

The pieces of furniture were few, but by far the most elegant Fane had ever seen, a teak desk with brass inlay by an open-mouthed sack of dried beans, a few chairs of rosewood or cherry. Doc Blount himself, a slender elderly man wearing spidery spectacles, busy at the moment of their arrival, moving up another sack of beans, said, "First of all, gentlemen, how about a little dram of something to settle the dust in your throats?"

Crezavent said, "That would be fine."

"No, thank you," said Arapaho.

Doc Blount's voice was calm, gave you the feeling he was well educated, and had a faint eastern accent, far eastern, seaboard. Fane liked him and couldn't help showing it. Crezavent didn't, and made no attempt to hide his antipathy.

Crezavent said, "Being Justice of Peace must pay well enough. As a tradin' post, this is just about the poorest I ever seen."

"The big trading post is in town," said Doc Blount. "Indians are pretty domesticated these days, and the country is just about hunted and trapped out. I don't have many customers, but the few Indians who deal with me are friends, and I mean just that. If they're honest with me, I'm honest with them." He pointed to the peltry in the storage space. "See that fine lynx? That, among others, was brought down from Canada by a couple of mighty close Indian friends of mine."

"From Canada!" said Fane amazed.

"What's distance to a Canadian Indian?" asked Doc Blount. "What can I do for you? A little tobacco, perhaps? I just have some pretty coarse twist."

Fane, who couldn't let the subject rest, said, "Where did you come from, and how did you wind up here?"

"Where I came from is none of your business," said Doc Blount, amused. "I wound up here because I was headed for Oregon and ran out of lucre."

Arapaho said, "You're a Justice of Peace. A Justice of Peace is a committing magistrate. He can hold his little court, he can issue warrants of arrest, or he can, if he thinks necessary, commit offenders to the grand jury."

"His powers, while limited in their scope," said Doc Blount, "encompass quite a variety of responsibilities."

This, decided Fane, was quite a nice sentence saying nothing. He realized, for a certainty, that this man was no fool.

Arapaho said amiably, "This is a court of law, isn't it?"

"So I've deceived myself into believing," said Doc Blount.

"And things that happen in a court become public knowledge, don't they?" asked Arapaho. "Open to me, or anybody else? That's the law, isn't it?"

"Is that so?" asked Doc Blount, looking interested. "I probably don't know as much about the law as I should. But I always enjoy hearing it gossiped about."

"I want to know about a lady that come up before you once," said Arapaho. "At least I'm pretty sure she did. I want to know all about it."

"What lady, may I enquire?" said Doc Blount.

"Miss Maribelle Browne."

"Yes, I remember, I think," said Doc Blount. "But when, as you mentioned, the public sees official records, I mean at courthouses and big places like that, aren't fees sometimes charged?"

"I'm willing to fork up any reasonable fee," said Arapaho.

"But the difficulty is;" said Doc Blount, pretending to look unhappy, "I don't keep records. Oh, I keep them, of course, because that very law you keep talking about demands it. But I keep them too well, you might say, I mislay them." He frowned, put a fingertip to his lower lip and added, "But maybe I can help you from memory. The trouble here is I seem to mislay my memory now and then, too. But we'll cross that bridge when we come to it."

"Did you write out a warrant for her?" asked Arapaho.

"Yes, I'd say so."

"Was it ever served on her?"

"I served it myself. I must have. As soon as I wrote it out."

"Did the sheriff follow it up?" demanded Crezavent.

"I'm afraid that's outside my province," said Doc Blount humbly.

"Was it for a felony?" asked Arapaho.

"Miss Maribelle?" said Doc Blount. "Oh, I hardly think so."

"Then what was it?" asked Fane. "That's the whole purpose of our visit, to find out what it was. We have been told our lives could depend upon this knowledge."

"All human lives depend upon something very ephemeral," said Doc Blount, completely unruffled. "That's a bitter lesson I learned many years ago."

"Do you want to help us?" asked Fane curtly.

"Not particularly," said Doc Blount. "The three of you bring a slaughterhouse odor into my living room with you. For one thing, I wouldn't wager a copper cent I'm even on my feet and breathing when you leave."

He's a brave man, too, thought Fane.

Yet, somehow there seemed to be a sort of half communication between this man and Arapaho.

Arapaho said, "You've earned no fee. I think I might as well tell you that at this point, before we leave. Leave you unslaughtered, by the way. But would you care to tell me anything at all that you can remember of it?"

"Could it have been a misdemeanor of some sort?" said Doc Blount. "That doesn't seem exactly right, but somehow I seem to classify it in a general way as a misdemeanor."

"No help at all — a waste of time," said Crezavent as they crossed the pole bridge over the creek and headed back to town.

Arapaho made no answer to this.

Each of the three men, as they returned to town, figured the time from the moon's position and the stars, and came to a general conclusion that it must be somewhere about eleven o'clock. This was a special kind of hour in any tough town. The peaceful citizens — and most of them were peaceful — the peaceful citizens had been sieved off the streets and had been at home sawing wood in their dirty underwear and long

120

nightshirts in their beds for a couple of hours, and would stay that way until their backyard fowl, hens as well as roosters, cut loose to greet the rising sun.

The amblers on the walks, while mighty thinned out, were not deserted, but Fane knew that about anyone you passed, likely, was a night-lifter, a tinhorn, a badman, or a sharpster — or just a rotgut-happy loafer who didn't care at the moment if a rooster, any rooster, crowed in the morning, ever again.

That was why they were so surprised, knowing this, all three of them to run into the situation by the watering trough.

The best and most popular of several public watering troughs in town was the one before The Stockman's Rest saloon. It was preferred by many because it was centrally located in the most decent business section of town, and because there was generally good light here, all through the night, from expensive saloon windows. The trough itself, just below the walk in the street, was a water-tight wooden box on a low trestle, fed at one end by a pump, cast iron, with a cast-iron handle. When the water was too low, or too fouled, you got fresh water by pumping it in yourself. A dipper hung from a wire hook on the pump, a dipper much used.

What surprised them was that Linda Southworth was just finishing pumping, and her father, having just filled the dipper, was drinking. There was no one else near, either on the walk or idling in any doorway. What surprised them was the danger of the hour, despite the fact that a glimpse of brass cartridges and a gun belt buckle could be seen in the inverted V below the buttons at the front of the rancher's coat.

That was the first thing Fane noticed, and that Mr. Southworth wore his gun belt high, old style, rancher's style, gentleman style. The second thing noticed by Fane was a buck-board a short distance away, just beyond the lip of light, loaded. The Southworths were on their way home, Fane decided, and Mr. Southworth was quenching his thirst, getting harmlessly fortified, just before they departed.

They themselves were still back in the edge of shadow, walking forward, when it happened.

Freneau came out of the door of The Stockman's Rest, with his night barman at his shoulder; each had his hands empty.

Making a loose-lipped, doughy, sensuous mouth, Freneau said, "So you have set your scabby curs on me, have you, you son of a bitch? Get out that gun!"

Southworth, startled, with his dipper chest high, said, "What?"

And Freneau, with mighty clumsy cross-draw, shot him. The gun roared like a cannon.

Southworth half spun beneath the hammer blow, the dipper went flying. Then the rancher, jaws ghastly slack, lay spread-eagled on the earth, eyes glazed, blood making a sickening paste of the ground by his half clenched fingers.

"He was carrying no gun, and you knew it," said Linda Southworth. "It's on the seat of the buckboard. You and the sheriff were on the courthouse steps ten minutes ago when I made him hand it over to me."

Arapaho, Crezavent, and Fane, came to a halt.

Pretending, and doing a pretty poor job of pretending consternation, Freneau said, "But the gun belt. He was wearing a gun belt!"

"You were there," said Linda, now bending over her father.

At that instant, Freneau, noticing the presence of Fane and his companions, melted to a helpless flabbiness.

"I'm in this," rasped Crezavent, but Arapaho, holding his hand flat out, commanded, "Hold it!"

An eerie thing happened. Southworth, with great difficulty at first, started to talk. He said, "Bring up that keg, Linda. And put it in front of me, on its side."

There was an empty nail keg by the board walk; she did as she had been ordered.

A look of grisly fright came over Freneau's face. He turned back toward the saloon. Arapaho frigidly said, "Stand as you were, Mr. Freneau."

"My gun, Linda, please," said Southworth.

She brought the six-shooter from the buckboard and handed it to him. He took it in his left hand. They saw he had been shot in the right shoulder.

With great torture, he rolled half over, rested the gun barrel on the keg's side, and said, "Try again, sir."

Freneau began to quiver and drool.

Southworth blasted him. Later, Crezavent was to say delightedly, "Right in his big fat mouth!"

Ten minutes later a doctor said, "He'll have a perished right arm, likely, but he could well outlive us all."

Linda said, "Somebody get a feather bed for a mattress and help me put him in the buckboard. I must get him to the ranch."

Arapaho said firmly, "He can't stand the trip. You'd better take him to the hotel."

"You people stay out of this," said the doctor. "The instant that chunk of lead smashed into his shoulder, he became my baby, and nobody else's. He goes home with me. To my spare bedroom — to my wife, who, over the years has become almost as good a doctor as me, and a little better better maybe, though I'd hate to have the fact know-rated around."

When Southworth had gone, and Linda, too, with the helpful hands that carried him, and they were for a moment alone, Arapaho said, "Ten inches can be a funny thing."

Freneau had been removed, and the barman was again inside, polishing glasses.

"Yes," said Arapaho thoughtfully. "Ten inches south-by-southeast and Mr. Southworth would be dead and our agreement with him null and void as of this instant. And me and Crezavent would be moving somewheres else, and Joe Fane would be cuttin' the mustard at a gallop, I'd bet, for Iraville. But no such thing happened. My!"

"I'm afraid I can't follow your line of reasoning," said Fane. "You explain it and explain it, and turn it every way but loose. It's over now, finished, and nobody can make it out any other way. Southworth's alive, so we're still working for him, I'll grant you that. But Freneau's dead, so who are we working *against*?"

124

"Let's hook our thumbs to our hammerspurs, and go ask Miss Maribelle," said Arapaho. "She ain't no barber from Yuma, like the Brothers Freneau, but she manages to get by all right, especially seeing she was picked up stranded at the railroad station in the first place."

CHAPTER
THIRTEEN

That rare but generally pleasurable summer phenomenon, a rain gale, was making up as they walked down Front, and slabs of black clouds were piling in from the west, wiping out the moon, making the street a channel, swallowing with blackness eaves and cornices and chimneys above their heads.

They passed the glorified alley which was Oak Street, and came to Miss Maribelle's warehouse-domicile-millinery. It stood there, its two stark stories of brick facing the railroad, four golden windows upstairs, four down, tinkling piano music as before, everything merry enough, yet somehow giving off a sinister effect. And now the first rain came down, a thin scattering only, with drops as big as silver dollars, cool and explosive, striking the backs of their necks and between their fingers as they entered.

A woman came up to them, a roly-poly little woman built like three pumpkins placed one on top of the other. She came up with a swirl of necklaces and bracelets and throwing off a fragrance which Arapaho later said was sandalwood but Crezavent swore was vanilla, and said, "Well, boys, welcome home. Come in and set around the campfire."

"Campfire?" said Crezavent. "I'd be jest as happy if I never saw another campfire."

"That's jest a homey manner o' speakin," said the woman, a stranger to them.

"We'd like a word with Miss Maribelle," said Arapaho.

"Miss Maribelle is no longer here," said the woman. "I've took her place. I'm Miss Annabelle."

"When did she leave?" asked Arapaho.

"Shortly, very shortly after Mr. Freneau met with his demise," said the woman. "Wasn't it sad?" They waited for more details.

"Vancouver," said the woman. "Terrible, terrible far away. Caught the 11:37. Three trunks, a portmanteau, and four bandboxes.

"Who took this luggage to the station?" asked Arapaho.

"Hickman Hauling," said the woman, and she said it so promptly they knew this must be a verifiable fact.

They thanked her, and with some difficulty managed to get away from her. Hickman Hauling was just next door; they had noticed it before. The sleepy nightman, after much summoning said he himself had seen them put on the 11:37.

The nightman at the station said he'd seen her get on. In fact, he'd helped her get on; she had been so faint he'd eased her aboard and into a parlor car, and handed her her bottle of smelling salts.

There was a bench on the platform, just to the left of the station door, much used in daylight but empty now; the time through the station window, from the big wooden octagonal clock now said 12:17. They seated themselves to get collected, to get organized, and

Arapaho said, "Well, I suppose it's only fair to admit it. I figured this thing wrong. And maybe Fane figured it right. It is over."

They waited.

"The feeling has been growing on me," said Arapaho, "that Miss Maribelle was the one planning to take over this whole thing. I'd bet a cigar she's the one, if you could get right down to it, who has been doing the actual managing all along, the brainwork."

The big raindrops had ceased. The air, coming in little rolling puffs, was cool. The gale, Fane decided, could very well move over. At this stage, it was hard to tell. It could be a cloudburst, or no water at all.

"You mean," said Crezavent, "that this Miss Maribelle just stirred up things between them, so they would kill each other off?"

"But how would that help her?" asked Fane. "It would be the Freneau heirs, and the Southworth heirs, who would own the businesses. We know for a fact, for instance, that Miss Linda Southworth would come in for her share. Her father told us so, and I believe him."

"The property, the real property, the buildings and equipment and such," said Arapaho, "amount to nothing in the kind of businesses they run, when you come down to hard facts. You could have tables and chairs, and bars with the fanciest backbars you could dream of — empty. Empty. No customers. Every restaurant, every saloon, knows this. It's how places are run, with a touch of something no one understands, that says whether they catch on or not. And it's my bet that it was neither of the Freneaus, or Mr. Southworth, even, who had that extra, necessary touch. It was Miss Maribelle Browne who had it; she knew gambling, girls, and liquor inside out, I'll bet. And Polton, when she realized it, was a ripe plum to her."

They got up, left the platform, and started across the road. A man came forward toward them, from the shadows of Front Street, into the bloom of light from the station windows behind them. He approached them cautiously, his hands held toward them, palms out, as though he were fending them off.

At first they didn't recognize him, grizzled, bow-legged. They came to a slow stop. Arapaho said, "It's Lyman Jones, that blacksmith."

Jones himself came to a halt a few feet in front of them.

"I want to talk to you," he said antagonistically.

"I don't want to hear anything you've got to say," declared Arapaho.

"Teddy Clark sent me," said Jones. "He wants to know if you could let him and his boys have some money? Just a little."

"Do my ears betray me?" said Crezavent.

"Freneau's dead, and they want to get out of town. And don't want to waste no time on it. He was stingy with money. He got 'em cheap drunk, gave 'em part of their pay, and promised them the balance in a big chunk with a bonus when the job was finished."

"And now he's dead," said Arapaho.

"Dead," said Jones.

"We want no traffic with them," said Arapaho.

All in all, Fane knew this wasn't as outlandish a request as it seemed on the surface. Gamblers, he'd heard, even mortal enemies, would stake each other in hostile towns in desperate circumstances.

Before he had left Iraville, his wife had sewn hastily into the waistband of his pants five hundred dollars on double eagles. This was an old, very old, immigrant's trick. He had taken it along to help up at Split Butte, if Baldecker should have financial difficulties along with his other trouble.

"How much do they need?" asked Fane, just talking.

"From here to Old Mexico," said Jones. "Whatever that is."

"Old Mexico?" said Crezavent, and horselaughed. "That I greatly doubt. Nothing could force them boys that far away. They're boys that circulate, and merchandise as they go."

Fane was thinking it would be pretty nice to close this thing up quick, and was about to say something, he wasn't sure just what, when Crezavent surprised just about everyone. He said, "I'm not too flush, but would fifty dollars help?"

"It's not much," said Jones. "But it would help a heap."

"One thing, though," said Crezavent. "I want to hand it over to Teddy Clark face-to-face, and be shore he gits it. I hear he's always debt-good."

"That would be okay with him," said Jones. "I have a feeling he'll want to thank you face-to-face."

They went up the sidewalk of Front Street, Jones a little in the front, leading them. They watched him like hawks.

130

They had gone about a half block, past darkened store windows, when they came to two, one-story buildings set back a dozen feet from the walk. Once they had been lump coal and baled hay establishments, probably, but were abandoned, one even with a broken windowpane. Between them was a passage, or rather through them, for it was a part of the same general rambling edifice. A watery tint of faint yellow light came from the passage mouth.

Jones entered the passage; they followed him, Fane's nerves atingle. About a third of the way down the passage's length, they came up to the light itself, a barn lantern. Teddy Clark was seated on the doorstep of a side door of one of the buildings — the lantern on the ground in front of him, slightly to one side.

As the light struck him from below, under his chin, under his cheeks, his face looked doubly doglike and vicious. He got to his feet and walked forward. Jones left the group and retraced his way a short distance up the passage toward the street, and stood.

From their group, Fane saw Crezavent step forward toward Teddy Clark. He said, "Teddy, I hate your guts, but you can have a little money if you want it. But you don't. Do you?"

"No," said Teddy Clark. "I want you."

"I'm a little harder to get than my money," said Crezavent almost tenderly.

And then, in a blasting of thunderclaps hammering against the sides of the passage, Crezavent was dead. Not only on the ground, dead, but meat grinder dead.

And it wasn't Teddy Clark who killed him, but Lyman Jones, up the passage, who, with attention distracted from him, had all the time in the world.

And Teddy Clark was dead, from Arapaho's single shot, also on the earth, not still like Crezavent, but threshing into eternity.

And after him, Jones lay crumpled, also from Arapaho's gun, from that weapon with the crosshatched butt, the gun which had started Fane into all this.

And if Jones were there, between them and the passage mouth, blocking them, there must be others backing him up this trap, the Flenner boys and Deluxe Harrigan.

Three against two; not impossible odds, but the situation was blind and terrible.

"Come on," said Arapaho, starting down the passage toward the passage interior at a lope. "Let's pick a better place. Let's know how things stand."

Gasping as he increased speed, he added, "No offense, but the idea was to have Jones wipe out Crezavent, from behind him. Teddy Clark thought he could take me straight, in which he was mistaken. That would leave only you. And then they could hunt you down like hounds after a rabbit."

But that was only part of the idea, they realized instantly. The rest of the idea was to get what remnants there might be left to do just what they were doing — to rush down the dark passage, the lantern light at their backs.

Fane's gun, too late, had come out of its leather back at the showdown. Now he held it loosely as he ran.

132

Three figures loomed up ahead of them directly in their path and the passage sides once again reverberated with an inferno of pounding gunshots.

One of the three figures broke and ran. The other two somehow were now limp on the earth, motionless. These two proved to be the Flenner boys, Blue Ash and Buddy. Later, Arapaho said, "The runaway must have been Deluxe Harrigan, off, after all, to a trip to Old Mexico."

"I wonder which one of us killed who?" asked Fane.

"We both got empty guns at the moment," said Arapaho. "We'll never know."

But Arapaho was just trying to soften it for him, Fane realized. Like saying one man in a firing squad was using a blank cartridge, to ease everyone's conscience later.

But one thing bore down on Fane's mind: he might be a slow draw, but he'd always been a crazy accurate shot.

Sheriff Sandy Sanderson's kitchen was pleasant and homey. They stood around the kitchen table with its big lamp, the sheriff and his wife, Miss Amanda, a sprightly little woman with determined eyes, their children, Fane, and Arapaho. On the table lay a large wallet, open. In front of it lay a sheaf of papers which the sheriff had spread fanwise, like a poker hand. He said, "We took it off his body."

Neither Fane nor Arapaho, waiting, said anything.

First, the sheriff removed three papers and shook them. "Leases to buildings now empty. One of them a pretty big one. What would a half-poor blacksmith be wanting with such?"

"Two of them could be a new Eclipse and a new Stockman's Rest, under different names likely, and the third, the big one, could be a new millinery shop."

"It don't make sense," said the sheriff.

"It does to me," said Arapaho. They waited for him to speak further. "Who knows?" said Arapaho. "Maybe the others would close soon from lack of trade."

"Lissen," said Sheriff Sanderson. "I've ordered you boys out of town, and tried to scare you out of town. Now I'll ask it as a favor."

"If you put it that way," said Arapaho, grinning, "yessir!"

"I mean *now*," said the sheriff.

"Yessir," said Arapaho.

Fane said, "First, would you shake hands with us?"

Startled, the sheriff said, "Why?"

"Because I'd consider it an honor," said Fane. "Because I consider you a mighty good sheriff."

"If you put it that way," said the sheriff, "what can I lose." He thrust out his paw. They shook hands all around, even with Miss Amanda.

"I've got some passable apple pie in my window box," said Miss Amanda.

"It sounds mighty good," said Arapaho. "But we're travelin'."

"One thing more," put in the sheriff. "We searched Jones' living quarters at his blacksmith shop. Over his pallet was hung a small picture. A litho of a butterfly asippin' from a dew-wet rose."

"He must have had a beautiful nature if you went deep enough," said Arapaho stolidly.

134

The sheriff continued; "It seemed kind of out of place. So we took it down and took it out of the frame, and in the back was a marriage certificate. Signed by Blount, the J.P., and witnessed by a couple of up-county trappers. Mr. Lyman Jones was hitched to Miss Maribelle Browne."

"But there was no record of it here at the courthouse?" said Arapaho.

"No, but I'm sure it was perfectly legal," said the sheriff. "You've heard how someplaces you can get hitched by jumping over a broomstick? Well, in this county you can just about get hitched by saying Simon-says-thumbs-up. If this is so, why did Miss Maribelle leave?"

"One thing you can bet on," said Arapaho. "She intended coming back again. As soon as this all blew over, I'd say."

Sunset spread like a shattered ember on the edge of the western prairie shelf when they cantered into Iraville, stiff, hungry, and parched.

Betty welcomed them with such equal enthusiasm that you would almost have thought Arapaho was a lifelong friend.

The Fanes had a neighbor who made it a practice to always keep at least two watermelons in a sack in his well, to chill them core-deep. After supper they put three chairs against the side of the store and ate one in the refreshing cool of the twilight.

Afterwards, when the men talked and told her what they had been through, Betty sat in the growing night and quietly listened.

Arapaho said, "Now there can't be much doubt about it. Lyman, a hard case if I ever saw one, must have been the Freneau general handyman for some time. He and this Miss Maribelle got their heads together and decided to set up a little competition, and they could have done it too. My guess says it was Lyman himself who killed that Ernie Freneau and fired up Fred to start the big trouble. The idea was to get the other two partners killed and clean the slate against him, and you can bet they'd get killed, too, some way or other."

Betty, when the conversation dwindled, said, "Arapaho — that's all I know what to call you, Arapaho — there's fine grazing around Iraville. Why don't you start a little spread of your own? Joe and I will stand behind you."

"Thank you kindly, but no," said Arapaho. "I know you're friends o' mine, and I don't have many, but I'll have to move."

"Just spend the night and stay for breakfast, then," said Fane.

"By breakfast, I'll be miles away. The night I'll spend out at that old stage station where we first met, Joe. I'll be in the saddle and not enough daylight to see the dust behind me long before you've laid out your small change for your day's trade."

Now Betty really put on the pressure. She said, "There are a lot of wonderful girls in town, hope chests all filled and perfumed with lavender, just waiting for the right man."

"I hear they're very popular these days," said Arapaho kindly, "weddings, and such goings on. But I must leave."

Obstinately, Fane came back to the main subject. He said, "How can you be so certain it was Lyman?"

Patiently, Arapaho said, "What happened up at Split Butte when your friend and his neighbor came to an agreement? The whole war went into nothing, immediately, and the out of county gunslingers, the non-locals, you might say, hauled out. The payroll was cancelled and the run of the mill gunthrower fights for one thing only — the hard dollar. Then why didn't it happen when Fred Freneau was killed? Because, maybe, the job wasn't finished. Because, maybe, someone was paying Teddy Clark and his boys to stay on and finish it."

"Lyman Jones?" said Fane, now convinced.

"He set up the trap for us *afterwards*, didn't he? Set it up, led us into it, and shot down Crezavent like the world depended on it."

They listened in silence.

"Take the way he shot Crezavent," said Arapaho. "He jest kept shooting him, after he was dead, to make sure."

Subdued, Fane said, "I didn't notice."

"I did," said Arapaho. "You've got to notice things like that."

ISIS publish a wide range of books in large print, from fiction to biography. Any suggestions for books you would like to see in large print or audio are always welcome. Please send to the Editorial Department at:

ISIS Publishing Limited
7 Centremead
Osney Mead
Oxford OX2 0ES

A full list of titles is available free of charge from:

Ulverscroft Large Print Books Limited

(UK)
The Green
Bradgate Road, Anstey
Leicester LE7 7FU
Tel: (0116) 236 4325

(Australia)
P.O. Box 314
St Leonards
NSW 1590
Tel: (02) 9436 2622

(USA)
P.O. Box 1230
West Seneca
N.Y. 14224-1230
Tel: (716) 674 4270

(Canada)
P.O. Box 80038
Burlington
Ontario L7L 6B1
Tel: (905) 637 8734

(New Zealand)
P.O. Box 456
Feilding
Tel: (06) 323 6828

Details of **ISIS** complete and unabridged audio books are also available from these offices. Alternatively, contact your local library for details of their collection of **ISIS** large print and unabridged audio books.